"Keeley, I had to see you."

Linc spoke again before she found her voice. "Please, don't send me away."

At his plea, her green eyes flew open and collided with his warm blue ones. Pulled together by a force neither one could deny, they found themselves moving closer.

Suddenly Linc stopped short. Stunned by his apparent rejection, Keeley winced and stepped back. "I think you'd better go," she blurted out. Her voice trembled in spite of her efforts to keep it steady.

"No! I won't go," he said harshly. "I can't go, not yet, not until we've talked."

"There's nothing left to say."

"Oh, I think there's a lot," he countered softly. And his eyes were saying it.

"Ms. Baxter sure knows how to hook her readers." —*Rendezvous*

MARY LYNN BAXTER

AUTUMN AWAKENING

MIRA BOOKS

ISBN 1-55166-300-7

AUTUMN AWAKENING

Copyright © 1983 by Mary Lynn Baxter.

Printed in U.S.A.

To my parents, for their love and support

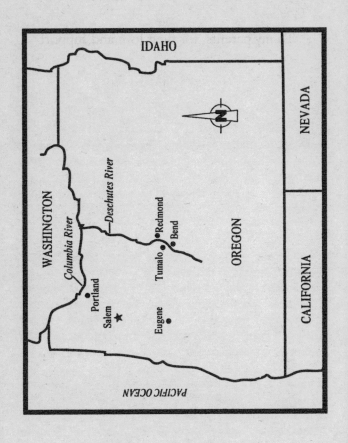

One

Keeley Sanders longed to be anywhere other than in this overheated room filled with athletes and coaches who proudly wore both their muscles and achievements like a second skin. Rowdy parties of this type only served to bring unpleasant memories to mind. But she had promised Luther, her father, that she would take his place at this function celebrating the end of spring training and the beginning of the professional football season.

Suddenly she felt prickles of uneasiness slide down her back. No matter how hard she tried, she couldn't shake the feeling that she was being watched, that her every movement was being closely scrutinized.

She scanned the room another time, trying her best to appear casual, not wanting to call attention to her paranoia, hoping to catch the culprit who was watching her. But again, she came up empty-handed. Her darting eyes saw only the crowd of people that filled the ballroom of the elite Portland Country Club to capacity. She closed her eyes and breathed deeply, wanting desperately to ease the sense of agitation that held her in its clutches.

"Ma'am, would you care for a drink?"

At the sound of a voice so close to her, Keeley jumped sideways and in doing so bumped the arm of the solemn-faced waiter hovering near her left shoulder. The tray he so delicately balanced now shook in retaliation, causing the bubbly liquid to spill from the glasses.

"Oh, please, I'm—I'm sorry. I didn't see you," Keeley sputtered as she tried to calm the now thoroughly harassed waiter. Giving her a lame smile, he quickly rebuffed her offer of help and then turned and headed back toward the bar to reload his tray.

A deep sigh escaped her lips as she forced herself to remain stationary until the waiter returned with the champagne. It wasn't that she really wanted the drink, but maybe it would help to conquer once and for all the feeling of unease that persisted. Also it would give her father's friends and co-workers proof that she was making an effort to join in the festivities.

Part of her reason for attending the party was to do some "PR" work, as Luther had put it. She shuddered, hating even the thought of smiling and making inane conversation with people she barely knew and, in some cases, didn't know at all. But she had to try.

If the team, of which Luther was seventy-five percent owner, didn't have a winning season this year, his other partner and two minor stockholders vowed to give him trouble, spelled in capital letters. They were blaming Luther for paying out big salaries to several of the players who hadn't as yet earned their "big" money. At this point in her life, her father certainly didn't need more trouble.

A man propped himself against the doorframe adjacent to the bar and watched the woman who sipped her champagne and kept glancing over her shoulder. Boredom always went hand in hand with these affairs, he thought. For a moment his escape lay in her, whoever she was, laughing now at something a friend had said. She was beautiful, beautiful in the truest sense of the word.

The color of her hair reminded him of strawberries and whipped cream mixed together creating a light shade of red. He noticed that it clung like shining silk to her delicately boned face before falling to gracefully brush the top of her coral-colored dress.

When she smiled, she was even lovelier. Perfect white teeth were the backdrop for an ivory complexion that was as clear as glass. He was too far away to see the exact color of her eyes, but he imagined them to be a sparkling green. She looked to be in her late twenties, judging from the experience and character that was evident in her face.

And her body. It was sensuous and exciting, he thought. Her dress clung in all the right places, emphasizing her perfectly proportioned legs, buttocks and breasts. His eyes stared with covetous interest at the steady rise and fall of those breasts. For an insane moment he wondered what it would be like to hold one of them in his hand. He felt the pulse in his throat begin to hammer. His palms were oozing sweat. Damn! Had he lost his mind? he asked himself. The last thing he needed was to become involved with a woman—any woman.

But it was too late. He was completely captivated by this one's alluring beauty and the sense of gentle breeding that surrounded her like a veil. He felt compelled to move closer. He watched. He wanted her.

Doris Martin's loud voice vibrated throughout the room. Her high-pitched tone claimed everyone's attention within hearing distance. ''Keeley Sanders! What on earth are you doing back here in Portland, especially in August? I didn't think anything could drag you away from Eugene and the university except a major catastrophe.''

Oh, no, Keeley groaned inwardly. What had she done to warrant being sought out by the biggest gossip in the football circuit? Forcing herself to smile, however, she replied, ''Hello, Doris. How've you been?''

''Can't complain. But tell me, seriously, what brings you back home?''

Keeley drew a deep breath. She loathed inquisitive people and resented any invasion of her privacy. This was one of the main reasons she hadn't wanted to come to the party. But she made sure none of her resentment showed.

''Actually, I've been back about three months now,'' she said. ''I just began the fall semester teaching early childhood classes at Portland State.''

Doris lifted perfectly arched eyebrows. ''Oh, really,'' she said. ''As I said before, I didn't think anything could ever drag you back this close to home and under your father's domination.''

Keeley held on to her temper with difficulty. ''As a matter of fact, I moved back to be near my father. He recently suffered another heart attack.'' She tried to cover her terseness with a smile through tight, stiff lips. She didn't think she was successful, though.

''Come on, Doris, be a sport and give Keeley a break,'' chimed in Angela Kincaid, Keeley's companion and longtime friend with whom she had been exchanging confidences before they were so rudely interrupted. Angela's husband was a sportswriter and was considered to be an important part of professional football's inner circle.

Doris flushed. "I didn't mean to pry, Keeley. It's—it's just that I know how you feel or felt about your father and..."

"Doris," Angela cut in briskly, "let's talk about your wedding. I hear it's going to be the event of the year." The warning in Angela's voice was unmistakable.

That was all the encouragement Doris needed. She proceeded to give a detailed account of everything from her bridesmaids' dresses to the exact color in each of their bouquets.

Keeley feigned an interest in order to keep Doris talking. She had no intention of answering any more of her questions. Her reasons for being in Portland were her own. She had already divulged more than she meant to. Angela too, she noticed, was content to let Doris talk about herself. She hoped that there would be time later for her and Angela to resume their visit.

While Keeley was listening to the drone of Doris's voice, she felt again that same prickling sense of uneasiness. She shivered. Paranoid or not, she was positive now that a pair of eyes was boring into her back. It seemed as if she were under a microscope. Deciding that the time had come to put a stop to this nuisance once and for all, she swiftly turned her head.

It was then that she saw him, a tall man standing nearby, staring at her with the hottest blue eyes she had ever seen. As their eyes locked, something vital and alive vibrated between them. Keeley had the sensation of being struck by a thunderbolt, so intense was her reaction to this man.

As he continued to hold her with his unwavering gaze she took in every detail of his appearance. His mane of sandy-colored hair was the backdrop for an angular face shaped with strong but finely carved features. Although his six-foot-plus frame was impressive, it was overshadowed by the pure muscle and brawn that cloaked his frame. He was dressed in a dark blue flannel suit that fell smoothly across his shoulders and tapered downward to mold his hips and thighs, leaving no doubt that a large man could wear clothes with both style and aplomb.

Keeley remained transfixed, unable to move. His eyes were still hot, so hot, and they said so much. She had never met a man whose eyes could devour her with such intensity. Suddenly, she felt a strange feeling attack her insides.

Good heavens! she thought. She was responding to this stranger like she was sweet sixteen and never been kissed, instead of a twenty-eight-year-old widow who had earned the right to call herself mature. But a little voice inside whispered: *You've come alive! For the first time in three years, you've come alive!*

But then a cold reality reasserted itself, shaking her to the very core of her being. What was the matter with her? Had she taken complete leave of her senses? She was long past the stage of being fascinated with athletes of any kind. Wasn't she?

With a force of sheer will, Keeley turned her eyes away from this man who for a moment had wielded the power to turn her calm and steady world upside down.

If someone hadn't approached him wanting his attention, Keeley guessed she would still be gaping at him with her heart hammering in her throat.

"Keeley, are you all right?"

Shaking her head as if to clear it, Keeley turned to

see Angela staring at her with furrowed brows. Keeley paused to sweep her hair away from her face, fighting for composure. "I—I, er, I'm fine."

"Are you sure?" Angela asked, her voice full of concern.

Keeley nodded hesitantly. "I'm sure, or at least I think so." Then why did she feel as if she'd had the breath knocked out of her? "Why don't we find us a spot away from all the smoke and talk some more," she added hurriedly. "I'm—I'm eager to find out what you've been up to." She was grasping for anything to keep her mind occupied.

Keeley was aware that her friend was more than a little curious about her strange behavior. But thank goodness Angela held her tongue and refrained from asking any questions. Anyway, how could she justify her behavior to anyone else, when she couldn't even justify it to herself?

Shortly, Keeley found herself sitting with Angela in one of the country club's many lounges, well away from the hubbub of the actual party. She should have been mixing and mingling with the football elite, but as the evening was still young, there remained plenty of time to do her father's bidding. If she had had her choice, though, she would leave this place, *and those eyes*, and return to her apartment where she felt safe and secure.

"Keeley Sanders, you haven't heard a word I've said, have you?" Angela was grinning, but Keeley could hear the frustration in her voice.

Keeley felt her face grow red from the neck up. "You're right, Angela, I haven't." She sighed deeply. "I'm sorry, but suddenly it seems as if my life has been turned upside down, and I'm powerless to do anything about it. Sounds crazy and scary as hell, doesn't it?''

"I don't want to pry, Keeley, but..." Angela let her voice play out, giving Keeley every opportunity to tell her to mind her own business. When she didn't, she plunged on. "Your problem wouldn't by any chance have anything to do with Linc Hunter? I couldn't help but notice your fascination with him. What's with you two, anyway?"

So that's *his* name, Keeley thought. Linc Hunter, Linc Hunter. The name kept circling her brain. Where had she heard that name before? Then it hit her with the same chilling effect as having a glass of cold water thrown in her face. *He* was the quarterback of the Portland Timberjacks, her father's professional football team. Keeley groaned inwardly. So that was the "famous" Linc Hunter! The same Linc Hunter her father was counting on to put the team in the winners' column.

He had made a name for himself in the sports world. Associating the name with the face brought to mind gossip she had heard concerning this very talented athlete. Not only was he the N.F.L.'s leading and most sought-after quarterback, but he was also the league's most sought-after bachelor.

"Good grief, Keeley, what's going on?" Angela demanded. "You're as white as a sheet. Did Linc Hunter put some kind of hex on you?" She smiled, but the smile never quite reached her eyes.

Keeley grimaced. "Not hardly," she snapped, then immediately regretted her sharp tongue after seeing the hurt look that crossed Angela's face. "Please, Angela, don't mind me. I'm just upset because I had to attend this party. Muscles and brawn have a way of setting my teeth on edge," she finished lamely.

Angela smiled. "You're certainly the exception to the rule, then, my friend." Her smile deepened. "Nine out of ten women I know would give their eyeteeth to have Linc Hunter look at them the way he looked at you."

"Well, they can have him and all the rest just like him for all I care," Keeley stressed. "He's good-looking all right, I'll admit that, but that's as far as *it* goes." Now why had she lied so blatantly? She wondered. Her heart was still thudding at a rapid pace from their recent encounter. She shuddered to think how she would react if she had to talk to him. But of course that would never happen, she assured herself.

"Considering what you've been through the last few years, I guess I can understand your feelings," Angela said softly. "But I could have sworn you weren't bitter...."

"Oh, I'm not," Keeley asserted quickly. "The bottom line reads like this: athletes as well as athletics are no longer a part of my life. Both my interests and life-style have changed completely since Paul died." She paused and sighed deeply. "The one thing that really bothers me about moving back and helping my father with his business affairs is the football team. I have to force myself to show an interest in it."

Angela nodded. "I can well imagine. Maybe, though, if you're lucky, you won't have too much to do that involves the team."

Keeley shrugged. "Let us hope."

"Since you are going to be here in Portland for a while," Angela said casually, "I want you to come and have dinner with Chad and me as soon as you can."

"I'd like that. Now that my father is a little better, I'm not quite so tied down. Of course, there's Judith, who absolutely dotes on Dad. She's always available to sit with him and actually spends more time with him than I do." She laughed, causing her face to come alive once more. "Dad forgets on purpose that I'm a working girl. He's beginning to give Aunt Judith a hard time about her job, too."

Angela grinned. "Your father's just spoiled, that's all. And in more ways than one!"

Keeley pursed her lips. "No one knows that better than I. Although, as you well know, I've made it a point to stay away from here and my father for a long time now. But since he almost died, I had no choice...."

"Of course, you didn't," Angela agreed instantly. "And sometimes it takes a tragedy to mend old hurts and pains."

"Time will tell. We'll just have to wait and see." Keeley smiled, striving to lighten the mood.

There was silence between them for a moment, and then Angela said with a smile of her own, "Keeley, I'd love to sit here and visit for the rest of the evening, but I can see Chad roaming around looking for me." She paused and stood up. "There're several people he wants to introduce me to. How about if I give you a call next week and set a definite time for dinner?"

Keeley nodded. "Sounds great. I'll talk to you then."

Now alone, Keeley wished she had another glass of champagne but didn't want to face the crowd to get it, so she quickly squelched the idea. If only this evening were over, she mused. Why had she promised her father she would come to this party? Because, she reminded herself harshly, he had wanted her to. And whatever Luther wanted, Luther usually got. In order to survive, he always had to have some poor soul at his beck and call. But for years now, it had been someone other than she.

She hadn't wanted to give up her job at the university in Eugene and move back to Portland, but at the time it was imperative that she do so. Her father was critically ill, not expected to live. He had suffered his second major heart attack. The fact that he had pulled through it was a miracle in itself, his doctors had told her. But they hadn't known how strong Luther's constitution was, or his will to live.

Judith, her mother's sister and the closest thing to a mother she'd ever known, pleaded with her to come back to Portland and help Luther with some of his business responsibilities. His very life depended on it, she said. So, under pressure, she had agreed to come home, refusing however to share the same house with her father. She rented an apartment and obtained a job at Portland State University teaching early childhood classes while he was too ill to argue. She was determined at all cost to maintain her hard-won independence.

"Care to have some more company?" a deep voice asked.

Keeley was brought back to reality with a jolt on hearing *his* voice. She knew without looking up that what she never expected or wanted to happen was indeed happening. Linc Hunter had sought her out.

Slowly she lifted her eyes to encounter his handsome face, now so very close to her own. As he tow-

ered above her, she could see the tiny lines based at
the corner of each eye. The rich odor of his cologne
drifted downward, causing her heart to increase its
beat.

"Hello," he said, a smile broadening his features.
"My name is Linc. Linc Hunter."

She should tell him to go away and leave her alone,
but her lips refused to obey and form the words.

Seeing the confusion reflected in her eyes, Linc immediately lowered his large frame onto the couch beside her, amusement shaping his eyes into small slits.

"I'm harmless, I promise," he said, cocking his
head to one side.

In spite of herself, Keeley smiled. "Something tells
me that's a lie, Mr. Hunter." Surely that hoarse sound
couldn't be coming from her throat.

He laughed. "Now what makes you think I'd lie,
Miss...?"

"Keeley Sanders, *Mrs.* Keeley Sanders," she said
pointedly.

His eyes fell instantly to her left hand. It was completely free of any rings.

"Why aren't you wearing a wedding ring, then?"

Keeley was taken aback at his bluntness.

"Well?" he pressed.

Tension hung thickly in the air between them. She
made a pretense of pushing her skirt forward, playing
for time. He was closer now, and she could see the
row of thick lashes that bordered his piercing blue
eyes.

"I'm not leaving until you answer my question,"
he said at last.

God! What arrogance! Keeley raised her clear
green eyes enhanced with golden flecks and stared at

him for a long time. Then, as if her mind and body were separate, she answered him, frostily, "I'm no longer married."

He seemed to relinquish the thin thread of tension that held his body taut. Then he hammered on, "Divorced?"

"No."

"Separated?"

"No."

"That only leaves one other possibility, then, doesn't it?"

Wordlessly she shook her head.

"I'm sorry," he said and meant it. Sympathy had softened his eyes and face.

"Thank you, but I lost my husband three years ago, so I'm no longer a grieving widow." If he thought her choice of words sounded cold and indifferent, he kept it to himself.

Instead, he said softly, "I'm glad."

Again, his simple statement threw her off balance. For a moment she was tempted to tell him who she was. She was positive that the knowledge that she was the boss's daughter would cool his heels. But in the long run what difference would it make? She had no intention of having any future dealings with Mr. Linc Hunter. So in order to save them both embarrassment, she would end this fiasco here and now.

Abruptly Keeley stood up, determined to leave. "I have to go," she mumbled.

"Please, don't go. Not yet. Stay and join me for a drink."

He watched intently as opposing emotions played across her face. Her eyes were large and perfect. He found himself drowning in them.

"Please," he repeated softly.

Keeley swallowed. "No, don't ask." Her voice was only a decibel above a whisper. "I—I need…"

"If you won't have a drink, then will you dance with me?" he cut in swiftly, pushing her further into a corner.

Keeley opened her mouth to argue but then closed it just as abruptly. The tumult that was building in her breast threatened to overwhelm her. She was attracted to Linc Hunter and could no longer deny it. But why? What did he have that so many others didn't? He had charisma, he had charm. But so did a lot of the other men she dated. Why, then, did she grow warm and tingly all over when she merely looked at him?

"Keeley?"

She gnawed at her lower lip for a moment longer. "If I dance with you this one time, will you leave me alone?" She looked him straight in the eye, daring him to challenge her.

He tossed her a light smile. "I'm making no promises, Keeley Sanders." Giving her no chance to respond to his overbearing attitude, he added, "Come on, let's dance," and gently propelled her toward the crowded floor.

Why, she wondered, was she letting him get the upper hand on her this way? Why didn't she just put him in his place and go on about her business? There again, she was plagued with questions, but strangely her mind shied away from delving too deeply for answers.

Reaching their destination, Linc's hand slid down her arm to her wrist; his fingers stroked her palms before interlacing them with hers. His eyes then circled meaningfully over the vee-necked bodice of her dress, lingering on the shadowy cleft between her breasts. Slowly, reverently, he drew her to him and molded her against his hard body. Keeley was positive he could hear her heart pounding erratically as she waited in trembling anticipation for his next move. As they joined together in harmonious rhythm to the sweet strains of Olivia Newton-John, Keeley gave herself up to the moment and stopped fighting the pleasure she found in his arms. His touch wielded a magic all its own. Suddenly she realized she was playing a dangerous game. Not wanting anything unpleasant to intrude on this moment, she pushed this unnerving thought aside and let herself feel only the subtle movement of his body.

"Keeley Sanders, whoever you are, you feel so good, smell so good and fit so well," he murmured huskily into her ear. The feel of his warm breath combined with his intimate words caused an unbelievable yearning to spread into her lower body. She had never felt this way before. No man had ever affected her senses this way, not even her husband—and she was afraid. Maybe it was a dream, this feeling of forbidden rapture that surrounded her. Maybe she would soon awaken and find herself curled up on the couch in her apartment reading a good book. But when she felt Linc's strong arm pull her closer, she knew her dream was very real.

"Please," she began, only to have her speech aborted by a throaty chuckle.

"Shhh," he commanded, "don't talk, just listen and feel. Feel the music that our bodies are making together."

Keeley Sanders! End this farce now! It had continued far too long as it was, she lectured herself. She shouldn't be dancing with this man in this manner; and more than that, she certainly shouldn't let him whisper sweet nothings in her ear.

But she simply could *not* disengage herself and walk away. It was beyond her power. It was as if she were glued to his hard, sinewy frame, so perfectly were they synchronized. They stayed like that, hardly moving, barely swaying to the music. Finally the song ended, and not a minute too soon for Keeley. Her emotions were stretched beyond their endurance.

As Linc guided her away from the dance floor, Keeley felt her nipples strain against her bra, seeking release from their confinement. She couldn't ever remember losing total control of her emotions and her body like this, not even after she had lost so much....

"Keeley?"

The low timbre of his voice brought her out of her stupor instantly. She looked up at him wide-eyed as she tried to control her breathing.

"Let's go somewhere, anywhere away from here," he ventured huskily. "Away from all these people." He paused as his eyes circled the room filled with faces and cigarette smoke. "I want to be alone with you." His voice held an urgency now. "We'll just talk. I don't care—you call the shots! I just want to be with you."

"No!" she stressed as her eyes searched avidly for the nearest ladies' room. She had to get away from Linc *now*. "Please, just leave me alone." Her eyes were wild as they pleaded with him. "You—you promised...."

A strange smile touched the hard curve of his mouth. "No, Keeley, you're mistaken. I didn't promise. I couldn't promise you then, nor can I now." His blue eyes stared at her intently, taking in the pallor of her face. "You look as if you could use a drink." A half smile softened his lips. "My offer still stands. How about it?"

She nodded mutely and found herself being led to the overcrowded bar. By the time they reached it, Keeley had come to the conclusion that she was handling *Mr. Athlete* in the wrong way. By refusing his demands, she merely increased his ardor and his determination. What if she humored him and played his game? Would he leave her alone and move on to bigger and better prey?

After their drinks were ordered, Keeley said, "If you'll excuse me, I need to go to the ladies' room. I'll be right back." Giving him no chance to respond, she darted in what she hoped was the right direction.

Keeley's hands shook as she repaired her makeup. What on earth had she gotten herself into this time? How could it be that she had attracted, of all people, the quarterback on her father's team? In all honesty, she had to admit that she was just as much to blame as he. With his raw masculinity, he had swept her off her feet—physical attraction of that kind was heady stuff. In spite of her convictions to the contrary, she was tempted to give in to this madness and accept his invitation. No! she cautioned herself. Her life was moving according to plan, and she didn't want or need any outside complications!

By the time she had smoothed the powder puff over her nose and glossed her lips, she felt much better, more composed. With her strawberry blond hair shining and a smile plastered across her lips, she made her way back to the bar with a whole new set of plans up her sleeve.

She noticed that during her absence a couple had joined Linc. Rather than disturb them, she decided that here was a perfect opportunity for her to melt into the crowd. She would speak hurriedly to Pete Rozelle, the football commissioner, and the others her father had urged her to see, and then slip away undetected.

At first it appeared that she would get away with it. But she made the mistake of looking in Linc's direction one last time. She was instantly caught and held by his piercing blue orbs. He smiled and waited.

She hesitated momentarily and then, with an agitated shrug of her shoulders and a smothered curse word, made her way toward him. The light touch of Linc's fingers on her skin as he drew her into the conversation caused a sharp spurt of electricity to shoot up her arm.

Linc smiled. "Joe and Margaret Barnes, I'd like for you to meet Keeley Sanders—a friend."

Keeley flashed him a stormy look before she turned and acknowledged the other couple.

The tall black-haired man smiled and shook her hand. "Pleased to meet you, Keeley," he said. His wife merely smiled and nodded to Keeley.

They stood and chatted a moment, not saying much of any importance. Keeley listened, contributing very little to the conversation. Her mind was elsewhere. It continued to gall her that she hadn't been able to get away from Linc. If only she hadn't cast that one last glance in his direction, she could very well be on her way home at this very minute. With a deep sigh, she forced herself to pay attention to what was being said around her.

It was obvious that the couple weren't close friends of Linc's. From what Keeley could gather, Joe Barnes was an executive with a sporting goods firm. But to her he was just another face, as were the countless others in the room. She was surrounded by faces that were foreign to her. She felt frustrated, angry. Even the people her father worked with were still strangers, the exceptions being his partner, Stan Engles, and his wife Millie. But she was determined to avoid *them* at all costs.

Since his illness, Luther trusted virtually no one. He refused to turn over any of the responsibility to anyone on his staff, least of all Stan. Luther's stubbornness certainly hadn't made for better working relations between the two men.

Instead he was insistent that Keeley be a part of every deal that was made, especially the important ones, and report to him. Her promise to do this was the only thing that kept her father quiet so that his heart could mend and become stronger.

"Keeley, your friend is trying to get your attention," Linc said softly, drawing her out of her reverie and back to the moment at hand.

A smile fleetingly crossed her mouth as she turned and saw Angela motioning for her. Keeley raised her hand, indicating she would join her shortly. When she turned back around, the Barneses were excusing themselves to move on to another group.

She felt Linc's warm gaze on her face. "I've about had it with this place. Please, if nothing else, let me take you home." His voice stopped short of pleading.

She swallowed. "No, Linc. I can't."

"Why?"

"That's none of your business," she answered sharply.

He sighed. "That's a cop-out, Keeley, and you know it."

"Believe me, Linc, it's no cop-out. It's the truth." Her voice sounded dead, even to her own ears.

"Damn it! Keeley—"

"Sorry, honey, I'm so late." A well-modulated voice interrupted his sentence. "I got tied up with a student and was late getting away." He leaned over and swiftly kissed Keeley on the lips.

For a moment Keeley couldn't move. *Jim! She had forgotten about Jim,* forgotten that he was to meet her here at the party. It dawned on her then what Angela was trying to tell her.

An uncomfortable silence fell between them. Linc remained motionless. Keeley saw a muscle in his jaw tense, and his eyes harden.

"Keeley, aren't you going to introduce me to *your* friend?" His voice was as hard as steel.

Keeley swallowed with difficulty. "Of course, I'm—I'm sorry." She paused, stiffening her shoulders as if she were heading into battle. "Linc Hunter, I'd like you to meet Jim Ellis, my—my fiancé."

Two

There was a stunned look on Linc's face as he stared first at Jim and then at her. Keeley felt her heart lock in her throat at the contempt laced with scorn she saw reflected in his eyes. She could not breathe, nor could she move. She was trapped in the misery of her own making.

The exchange of greeting between the two men was completely lost on Keeley as she bowed her head, fighting for composure. She blocked out the glacial hardness that now rested on Linc's features, replacing the other more violent emotions. She felt herself drowning in her own self-contempt. It was her fault that the whole episode happened in the first place. If she had done what was right and sent Linc away, she wouldn't be standing here now with a sick feeling in the pit of her stomach.

Jim tentatively touched her arm, drawing her out of her trance. When she looked up, she saw that Linc had disappeared. It was just as well, she told herself. There was nothing left to be said.

Jim's hand remained on her arm, gently caressing it as he vied for her attention. His touch sent a cold shiver dancing up and down her spine. Keeley found herself wanting to draw away from him, away from the whole situation. She felt like screaming.

"Honey, why don't we mill around for a minute and then leave." His eyes were warm and tender as they looked down at her. "I haven't seen you all week, and I hate to share you much longer with all these people."

Keeley smiled weakly. "There are a few people I need to touch base with, and then I promise I'll be ready to go." She could hear the tremor in her voice in spite of her efforts to keep it steady.

She cut her eyes quickly in Jim's direction to see if he noticed her agitation. But his face told her that he was totally unaware of any undercurrents whatsoever. She breathed a sigh of relief. When everything else failed, she could always depend on Jim. Strife and discord never seemed to touch him. He was as steady as the Rock of Gibraltar.

Keeley had met Jim Ellis at the university in Eugene when she began teaching there three years ago. They became good friends almost immediately. Even though he was the head of the education department and in actuality her boss, their interest in teaching drew them together, creating a common bond between them.

Although not handsome, his black hair and warm gray eyes fit his tall lanky frame to a tee. Many times Keeley had amusingly referred to him as the absent-minded professor.

Keeley had pondered long and hard before agreeing to become engaged to him. When she finally decided to do so, it was with the understanding that she did not love him as he loved her. However, she greatly admired and respected him. Jim was everything her husband hadn't been—dependable, kind and mature. He represented the security and stability which she craved. In time, she was positive her feelings for him would grow into a deep and abiding love. For Jim, this was promise enough. He was willing to take her on any terms.

Now as Keeley walked beside him, she longed to feel the surge of contentment that always surrounded her when she was with him. But tonight it just wouldn't come. For a moment, she found herself wishing her companion was a blue-eyed, sandy-haired man with a rakish grin. But treading on the heels of that thought came another one just as earthshaking: She must indeed be losing her mind if she could even contemplate exchanging Jim for someone who would only bring her pain and misery.

Reminding herself that there was more to life than physical attraction, she squeezed Jim's arm and gave him a bright smile. "I'm so glad you came," she said.

At first, she kept her eyes peeled for signs of Linc. But it was obvious, after a while, that he was no longer among the guests. This knowledge gave her the courage to stay long enough to make her father proud of her.

Midnight was the magic hour when Jim finally escorted her to the apartment. He didn't raise too much of a fuss when she pleaded fatigue as a reason for not letting him linger. He was extremely patient with her, never pushy or demanding, always the gentleman. So it was with a quick kiss and a promise of tomorrow that he left to make his way to the Holiday Inn where he always stayed while in Portland.

The trip to her father's house every Saturday was a ritual she had performed faithfully since moving back to Portland. The mornings were spent discussing business and the afternoons in taking long walks around the grounds of his luxurious home.

Years ago Luther had purchased an old mansion on the outskirts of the city and had had it completely refurbished. There were twenty acres of land with the house, which added to its beauty. Since then, much of the grounds had also been relandscaped, making it into quite a showplace. Since he had been ill, it had become a haven to him. Its quiet peace and serenity had a soothing effect on him that seemed at times to work better than medicine.

Keeley loved the gracious old house and enjoyed her visits, but that was as far as it went. There had been too much said and done between her and Luther that made it virtually impossible for them to live together under the same roof.

But it pleased her that he needed her now as he never had in the past. Except for handling the football team's business affairs, she took delight in helping him.

Keeley parked the car in the front of the house and got out. Making her way up the front steps, she noticed that the late August air was tinged with a breath of fall. She paused a moment to inhale the poignant odor.

A large woman, whose face was lined with smiles, stood framed in the doorway.

"Good morning, Marie," Keeley said with a grin. "How are you this beautiful day?"

"I'm just fine." Her eyes twinkled. "I have the batter made, and when you're ready, I'll dish up your pancakes."

Keeley smiled again. "Great! Let me check in with

Dad and Aunt Judith and I'll be there shortly." She paused momentarily. "Are they in the usual place?"

Marie nodded and smiled as she made her way back toward the kitchen. She had been her father's housekeeper and cook as long as Keeley could remember. She hovered over and took care of every member of the household.

Keeley walked through the living room and hall as she headed for the back of the house. Since his illness, Luther spent most of his time on the glassed-in porch that provided him with a perfect view of what he comically referred to as his empire. It was a charming room, painted a bright yellow, with plants in every corner. The furniture was white wicker with brightly colored lime-green cushions providing all the comfort one needed.

When she stepped through the passageway, she saw her father sitting in his favorite lounge chair in the process of placing the phone back in its cradle. She immediately took in the pallor of his skin, realizing just how lucky he was to be alive.

Luther Cooper looked up at his daughter with a frown denting his forehead. "Well, it's about time you got here!" he barked. "Don't you know what time it is, girl?"

Keeley hid a smile as she crossed the room and leaned down, giving him a peck on the cheek. She wasn't at all alarmed by his crotchetiness. The majority of it stemmed from his trying to cover up his dependency upon her and his delight in seeing her.

At fifty-eight, he looked to be in much better physical condition than he actually was. Two serious heart attacks would have gotten a lesser man down, but not Luther Cooper. When standing, he was a tall, slender man, with a mop of thick gray hair. His piercing green eyes were hooded by dark bushy eyebrows, and were the exact replica of his daughter's. The only visible signs of his ill health were the paleness of his face and the deeply etched lines around his mouth and eyes.

"Now, Dad, don't fuss so," Keeley said. "You knew I'd be here just as soon as I could." She reached down and adjusted the afghan across his lap. "I haven't let you down yet, have I?"

"Hell, no, but there's always a first time!"

Although his gruff voice said one thing, his twinkling eyes said another. Keeley knew he was teasing her. She played along and humored him.

A smile lurked at the corners of her mouth as she sat down opposite him. "Did you know that it's unusually chilly outside for this time of year?" she asked.

Luther looked at her with his sharp green eyes. "You bet I did. The smell of football is definitely in the air." He grinned wickedly.

Keeley groaned and rolled her eyes heavenward. "Dad, is football all you *ever* think about?"

"Huh!" he snorted. "I didn't know there was anything else *to* think about."

"You're absolutely impossible, you know," Keeley countered with a grin. "No wonder Aunt Judith throws up her hands in total despair." She paused as her eyes scanned the room. "Speaking of Aunt Judith, where is she?"

Luther gave an exasperated sigh. "She forgot and left some of those damned papers she has to grade at home. She said they had to be done by Monday, so she went to get them."

"Don't be too hard on her," Keeley admonished. "I know exactly how she feels. It's terrible when the ungraded papers begin to stack up."

"If I had my way, both of you would give up those time-consuming jobs."

Keeley groaned again. "And do what, cater to you?"

Luther grinned sheepishly. "Wouldn't be a bad idea, now that you mentioned it."

"Pooh!" Keeley replied. "That's what's wrong with you now. You're spoiled absolutely rotten."

"Who, me?" he teased. "You must have me mixed up with some other fellow."

Keeley laughed, enjoying this rare moment of camaraderie with her father. It was highly unusual for the hard and stern Luther Cooper to let his guard down long enough to indulge in this type of exchange.

Changing the subject, Keeley suggested, "Why don't you talk to me while I devour some of Marie's pancakes. I would wait for Aunt Judith, but I'm starving."

For the first time in many years, father and daughter walked together hand in hand to the dining room. It was times like this that made her more determined than ever to hurry up and marry Jim. She longed to have a home and family of her own. Luther, in his mellowing old age, would be a much better grandfather than he ever was a father. Down deep, Keeley felt she owed him a grandchild. Perhaps it was because he wanted it so much.

Keeley was halfway through her meal when Judith appeared in the doorway. "I'm sorry, Auntie," she said, swallowing a mouthful of pancakes, "but I couldn't wait another minute to feast on Marie's delights.''

Judith waved her hand, warding off further apology. "That's just fine, dear. I'm glad you didn't wait. If the truth be known, I don't need to eat anyway."

Keeley shook her head in mock despair as she looked at Judith Wells. There was not a hair out of place on her finely shaped head, nor was there an extra ounce of flesh on her frame. Of medium height and build with magnolia-tinted skin, it was hard to believe that she was already fifty-two years of age. The only visible sign marking her years was the flecks of gray nestled amidst her dark brown hair. She was the gentlest and kindest person Keeley had ever known, and she loved her deeply.

"Keeley, where's Jim?" Luther began. "I don't mind sharing you part of the day, but we have a good deal of business to cover today."

Keeley glanced down at the thin gold watch that circled her arm. "He'll probably be here about one o'clock to take me to lunch." She sighed. "He has to go back to Eugene this afternoon. There's a faculty party tonight, and he's obligated to be there. At the president's insistence, of course," she added hastily.

Judith frowned and patted her on the shoulder. "That's too bad, dear. It's a shame you two are so far apart. You really should consider getting married, you know."

"Tell her, Judith! Damn it, I've been trying to talk some sense into her for the past three months," Luther intervened with disgust. "And she still refuses to listen."

"Hey, you two, cut it out!" Keeley demanded. "Remember, I'm a great big girl now, who's perfectly capable of making my own decisions. Believe me, when I decide to get married, you'll be the first to know." She smiled, taking the edge off her voice. She then rose and covered the short distance to the kitchen where she deposited her plate in the sink.

Luther grumbled under his breath but, for once, held his tongue.

Judith followed her into the kitchen. "I'm sorry, honey," she said, a flush staining her cheeks. "You're right to tell us to mind our own business. It's just that we want the very best for you, and we think Jim *is* the best."

"I know." Keeley smiled shakily. "And I appreciate your concern. It's just that..." She let her voice trail off. What more could she say unless she told Judith about Linc? Heaven forbid! Under no circumstances could she do that!

"Keeley, honey, what's the matter?" Judith asked, following a moment of uneasy silence. "Remember, you can't hide your feelings from me. I've seen you through some rough times." Her voice was full of gentle concern.

"I—I know," Keeley gulped, busying her hands with the pretense of rinsing off the plate. "And I love you so much. I don't know what I'd do without you." She forced a smile and tried to lighten the mood. "Don't you ever get tired of taking care of me?"

This statement brought a wistful but warm smile to Judith's face, making her truly beautiful. "Never, my dear, never. From the moment you were born, you brought me untold joy. When your mother died a few hours after your birth, I didn't think Luther and I, either one, could stand it." Her eyes began to fill with tears. "Losing my only sister was like losing a part of myself. But when your father placed you in my arms, a tiny bundle so real and so demanding, I never looked back.'' She paused and wiped her tears. ''I promised to love you like the child Don and I never had and to give you the very best life had to offer.''

''And you did, too,'' Keeley stated softly, ''for which I'll always be eternally grateful.''

''I wouldn't take anything for those hours I spent molding and teaching your young, inquisitive mind,'' Judith went on as if Keeley hadn't spoken. ''I couldn't wait until the bell rang every day, dismissing my fifth-graders so I could rush home to you.''

Suddenly, Keeley felt a burning sensation at the back of her eyes as she leaned against the cabinet. ''If it hadn't been for you, I certainly don't know what would've happened to me. Dad was much too busy to care,'' she added with a trace of bitterness.

Judith's eyes darkened. ''Don't be too hard on your father for his past mistakes. He doted on your mother, and when she died he was devastated. In his own way, he loved you and still does, more than you'll ever know.''

Keeley sighed. ''Perhaps you're right. He made sure I had the very best things money could buy, including babysitters and private schools. But all I know right now is that we're both lucky to have you. Since Uncle Don died, you've become the mainstay of our family.''

She smiled. ''Oh, I wouldn't go that far, my dear.''

''I would, and further,'' Keeley said firmly. ''Just look how you stayed by Dad ever since his first heart attack. If it hadn't been for you, making him rest and take his medicine on time, he'd be dead right now. I'm convinced of that.''

Judith's eyes fluttered as she cast them toward the breakfast nook where Luther still sat reading the paper. "Oh, please don't say that. I—I couldn't bear it if anything..." She broke off quickly with a flush staining her cheeks. "Anyway," she went on hurriedly, "your father's on the road to recovery now and won't be needing me much longer." A smile crossed her lips, but her eyes remained deep pools of sadness.

"That's where you're wrong, Auntie," Keeley countered. "Even though Dad may not admit it, he depends on you a great deal and looks forward to your daily visits." And that was certainly no extension of the truth, Keeley thought. She didn't know what would become of Luther if he didn't have Judith. Keeley had also noticed the way her aunt sometimes looked at Luther, like now for instance, with wistfulness intermingled with longing reflected on her face. It made Keeley wonder....

"Hey, you two, what's going on in there?" Luther called, a grumpy sound to his voice.

Keeley laughed, breaking the tension. "Shall we go, Auntie, dear? The master has called."

Linking her arm through Keeley's, Judith said softly, "Keep in mind that my shoulder is always available when and if you need it."

Keeley sighed as she gave Judith's hand a grateful squeeze. How could she explain to either of them that her emotions were in shreds, that right now she couldn't contemplate marriage to Jim, that first she must conquer her sudden attraction for a certain blue-eyed, sandy-haired hunk, who had been on her mind constantly since last evening. She felt she was being deceitful, and hated herself for that feeling, but she was fresh out of ideas as to how to exorcise Linc Hunter from her mind.

By the time she settled next to her father on the couch, Keeley felt somewhat calmer. She forced herself to pay attention to what Luther was saying.

"Okay, I want you to give me a blow-by-blow account of the party." He paused, the grooves deepening around his mouth. "I still can't believe that the season begins in just one week, and I wasn't able to celebrate with my staff and friends." His voice was tinged with bitterness.

Keeley's eyes softened as she tried to help him overcome his feeling of helplessness. "Now, calm down, Dad. Don't get yourself all stirred up for nothing." She reached over and gave his arm a squeeze. "You're improving every day. Just try to exercise a little more patience, and one day you'll be good as new."

"Huh! We'll see," he replied gruffly. But she noticed that the tension had lessened somewhat around his mouth following her words of encouragement.

The next thirty minutes kept Keeley busy elaborating on the details of the party. Luther asked what seemed to her like a million questions concerning each guest in attendance. Keeley had never seen her father so inquisitive and concerned about a party that occurred every year and would continue to do so in the years to come. Where was the fascination? Then she realized with a jolt that this was the first time Luther was not at the helm of his empire. He wasn't in complete control. He was dependent upon others to do things for him, and he loathed being in that position. The reverse had always been the way of life for the powerful Luther Cooper; he was having a hard time adjusting.

When Luther seemed satisfied with what Keeley had told him, he made his way to his desk and turned to her with a list of things he wanted her to do. Some of it, she noted quickly as she scanned the page, had to do with transferring money from one account to another, insurance problems and several other items of minor importance for her to attend to. There was nothing on this list that pertained to the Timberjacks, for which she was thankful.

She did not mention one word to her father about her encounter with Linc Hunter. Nor did she intend to. If she handled the situation correctly, there would be no reason for him to ever find out about it.

"Well, Dad, does this about wrap everything up for now?" Keeley asked at length, laying the papers aside and standing up. She raised her arms above her head and stretched her cramped muscles.

"I certainly hope so," Judith cut in as she, too, stood up and stretched long and hard. During the time Keeley and Luther had been hard at work, Judith had stationed herself in a quiet corner and graded her school papers. "If you two don't hurry," she added, "you won't get your walk in today. It's almost time for Jim to get here."

"Don't worry, Aunt Judith," Keeley said. "It won't hurt Jim to wait. I'm not going to be able to eat another bite of anything right now anyway. I'm still stuffed from all those delicious pancakes and whipped cream!" She laughed and patted her flat stomach.

This comment drew another snort from Luther.

"You look to me like you're on the verge of drying up and blowing away."

Keeley grinned and pointedly ignored his last remark. It was a battle they had fought many times. Although thin, she was in good health, and that was all that mattered.

"If we have indeed taken care of everything that's important for today, then we might as well take our walk. It's such a gorgeous day and I'm eager to get outside and enjoy it."

"Sounds like a good idea to me," Luther responded as he stood up and reached for the light jacket hanging on the back of his chair. Then he turned suddenly back toward her. "Oh, before we go," he added, "there *is* one more thing." He slapped his forehead with his hand. "And here I was just about to forget to tell you. It's damned important too!"

Keeley frowned. "Well, let's have it. I'm listening." Out of habit she reached down and picked up the afghan that Luther had flung aside and began neatly folding it.

Luther cocked his head to one side and eyed her intently. "Remember when you came in, I was hanging up the phone?" Keeley nodded and he went on. "Well, the party on the other end was none other than Linc Hunter's agent and..."

Luther halted abruptly when he saw the incredulous look that appeared on Keeley's face.

"What's the matter, girl? Did I say something wrong? You look like you just saw a ghost."

Keeley felt a tremor shoot through her body as swiftly as an arrow. She breathed deeply, trying to maintain control. If the mere mention of his name could bring about such a reaction, then she was indeed in more trouble than she'd ever imagined. And she feared the worst was yet to come.

"Damn it, Keeley, what's the matter?" Luther bellowed, concern darkening his eyes.

Keeley swallowed hard. "Nothing—nothing," she stammered, "everything's fine." But everything wasn't fine. She felt sick.

Luther's eyes narrowed. "You couldn't prove it by me!"

"Go—go on. Don't mind me. Finish what you were saying." She sank weakly to her knees onto the nearest chair. She forced herself to pay close attention to his words in hopes of crushing the turmoil that boiled within her.

"If you're sure you're all right?" he said, but he looked far from convinced. Shaking his head, he continued. "I know you're not aware of it, but Linc Hunter *is* the team's pride and joy. It's on Linc's heels that we're going right into the Super Bowl and win it! And win it big!" His eyes gleamed with excitement. "But there's always a kink in every silver lining, unfortunately. In this case, it's Linc's contract. It runs out at the end of this year. We began negotiations sometime back, actually several months before I got sick again." He paused to clear his throat. "Anyway, to make a long story short, he's ready to continue the talks so..."

"But, but," Keeley interrupted, "I don't see what all this could possibly have to do with me." But she did. Her heart began hammering against her ribs, loud and strong.

"It has everything to do with you." He sounded exasperated. "If you'll let me finish, you'll find out."

Keeley drew a trembling breath. "All right," she said in a defeated tone.

"I've made arrangements for you to have dinner tonight with Linc Hunter to try to negotiate a contract, get his name on the dotted line once and for all. That is, if you can," he added, but with considerably less confidence.

"What!" Keeley half rose, a hand grasping nervously at her chest. "Have you lost your mind?"

This time Luther shot her a fulminating look but went on, "Negotiating contracts is one of the necessary evils that all owners or managers have to contend with at one time or another." He paused, brushing a hand across his forehead. "And this particular contract is extremely important to me. If I could get Hunter to sign up for another three years, maybe it would help get Stan off my back."

"If Linc Hunter is so great," Keeley shot back at him, "then tell me why the team's had three losing seasons in a row."

Luther's shoulders sagged in defeat. "Because, as you well know, several of the other key players haven't been doing their jobs. The quarterback can't do it all!" He paused and shifted his weight more comfortably in the chair. "But I feel this is the year we're going to turn it all around! From now on the Timberjacks will be a household word. That's why it's so damned important we don't lose Linc Hunter."

"But Dad—"

"You know I'd take care of it myself," he added reproachfully, "if I could."

Keeley knew he spoke the truth. His face had turned ashen in color, and the knuckles on his hands were white from gripping the chair in frustration. She felt a surge of guilt rush through her.

But at the same time she had an obligation to herself, and to Jim. She had to talk Luther out of this insane meeting. There was no way she could meet Linc Hunter again. And certainly not for anything as personal as dinner, even if it *was* for business purposes. She must convince Luther that she couldn't handle the assignment and do it as diplomatically as possible so as not to arouse any suspicions on his part. It wasn't going to be easy, though, not when that obstinate look she knew so well, pinched his features.

Keeley squared her shoulders. "Listen, Dad, you know I don't mind doing what I can to help, but in this case, you're asking too much of me." She paused, wetting her lips nervously. "I don't know the first thing about setting the terms for any contracts, much less how to bargain," she finished on what she hoped was a firm note.

Luther sighed and sank back onto his chair. "All I want you to do," he explained patiently, "is to listen to what Linc wants and take notes, or give him a pen and let him sign his name. It's that simple." His eyes bored into hers. "Now, you mean to tell me you can't handle that?"

Suddenly her hands and face were cold, and her stomach began to flip-flop. Push had indeed come to shove. What now? she asked herself. Could she do it? Of course she could, she argued with herself. She could do anything she had to. Maybe seeing Linc was a good idea after all. Maybe it was possible that her wild attraction to him was only a figment of her imagination. She was being given the opportunity to find out. Was she willing to risk it?

"Well, can I depend on you, girl?"

Keeley felt her throat close. She played for time. Her eyes quickly searched the room looking for one last avenue of support—Judith. But the minute their eyes met, she knew where her aunt's sympathies lay. In fact, her eyes actually pleaded with Keeley to indulge Luther and do as he asked. Keeley realized instantly that she had no choice. Luther was too ill to handle it himself. What other alternative did she have short of telling him the truth?

The silence in the room lengthened. Both her father and Judith stared at her with a puzzled look on their faces. She was aware that they thought she was behaving very strangely.

"What time?" Keeley asked, her voice tautly neutral.

Luther breathed a sigh of relief. "I knew you'd see it my way. It'll be a piece of cake. I bet you land us another three-year contract. He's ready to see things my way now, I'm sure of it. Anyway, Linc's to pick you up at your apartment about eight o'clock." His eyes gleamed with unsuppressed excitement, anticipating the sweet taste of victory.

Keeley felt as if the weight of the world rested squarely in the middle of her shoulders. It was all she could do to maintain a semblance of control in front of her father when she felt so trapped and defeated.

Finally their business was concluded, and they made their way outside to join the sunshine and the cool air. "I'll do the very best I can, Dad," Keeley said, squinting against the sudden light in her eyes. "But I'm not promising I can accomplish the miracle you're halfway expecting." She must make it clear that she might fail. It would help to soften the blow later.

"Oh, I don't know so much about that," Luther replied, throwing his arm around her shoulders and drawing her close. "I'm positive you won't let me down."

Keeley drew back and looked up at him with a scowl marring her features. "I still don't understand why Stan can't take care of all this. It seems to me the odds would be overwhelmingly in his favor. After all, he *is* your partner and general manager, and it just might help to calm him down."

Luther shook his head. "Don't want him or anyone else talking contract." His face became set and cold. "In spite of my incapacitation, I'm still determined to maintain control of the players through you."

If he only knew her reactions to one of the players, she thought, his star player at that, he wouldn't be so eager to involve her. Luther abhorred the idea of her becoming involved or fraternizing with any coach or athlete ever again. He was positive, after her unhappy marriage, that he didn't have anything to worry about on that score. And she had been equally as positive until she met Linc Hunter.

Suddenly, Luther stopped and peered into her face with hooded eyes. "You sound as if you're thinking of changing your mind."

Keeley kept her silence for a moment. "No—no. I won't change my mind," she replied hastily. "I gave you my word." *And I hope I won't live to regret it,* she added silently before jerking her body up straight and heading toward the house and Jim.

Three

"Why didn't you tell me who you were?"

Keeley squeezed the doorknob until she felt the circulation die in her hand. Linc Hunter's quiet but controlled voice did more to unnerve her than if he'd yelled at her for what he thought to be a master plot of deceit on her part.

He stood before her looking superbly fit and handsome in a dark blue pin-striped designer suit with a matching shirt and tie. The massive bulk of his shoulders almost took up the entire doorway, making it impossible to see anything other than his powerful body.

His eyes were the exact color of glazed blue marble as he stared at her with measured intensity.

Keeley felt shivers run down her arm as she took a tentative step backward. "Please—please, won't you come in?"

Removing his hands from his pockets, Linc moved with an easy-jointed grace across the threshold and into the softly lighted room. He never once took his eyes off her.

Keeley clenched her hands tightly together as she tried to think of something to say that would dispel the tension that hung over the room like a thick blanket of smog.

She had waited in dread for this moment all afternoon. After Jim had met her at Luther's, they had gone to a soup and salad restaurant where they enjoyed a light lunch. But her mind had kept wandering. She had sensed Jim's impatience with her, but as usual, he had refrained from saying anything.

Now the actual confrontation with Linc was every bit as difficult as she imagined it to be. She felt the same panicky feeling invade her body as when she had first met him. His lethal brand of charm was now even more potent as it drew her toward him. It was as if they had never been apart.

She saw all her good intentions for exorcising him from her mind go down the drain. She found herself back to square one—a position definitely not to her liking.

When she finally turned her gaze toward him, she felt her breath catch in her throat. His eyes were devouring pools of fire as they traveled over her face and the length of her body, never pausing to rest on any one spot for long. Heat flickered through her at an alarming rate of speed.

Oh, God, what was it about this man that could turn her bones to jelly and render her speechless? How could she let it happen all over again? she taunted herself. She stared at him with her feelings a tangle of resentment, frustration and bewilderment. The sooner she put this evening behind her, the better off she would be. She must never see Linc Hunter after this meeting. It was almost as if she were addicted to his eyes and his body. Anything *that* habit-forming needed to be done away with.

"Why didn't you tell me who you were?" he repeated softly, his eyes still refusing to release hers.

Keeley licked her dry lips and turned her back on him. "I—I didn't think it was important." She bit her lip to control its tremor. "I—I planned never to see you again."

He moved closer to her. She could smell the musk odor of his cologne; it was the same enticing fragrance he had worn the previous evening.

"You knew better than that," he replied, the timbre of his voice low and husky.

She shook her head. "No, no, I didn't know better than that," she stressed with effort.

Somehow she managed to make herself move to the other side of the room where she reached for her purse that lay confined between the cushions on the couch.

Turning, she faced him, determined now more than ever to put things back in their right perspective and behave like the sane, rational woman she knew herself to be. "I'm ready when you are," she said with a tight smile, her voice cool.

Keeley saw a slow answering smile cross Linc's lips, showing off his even white teeth to perfection. "You're beautiful, did you know that?"

Her heart took a downward plunge. She clutched her purse closer to her chest as if to ward off any further intimacies from him and answered defiantly, "So I've been told many times by my fiancé Jim." She knew she was using a childish ploy, but she was desperate to put him in his place—now.

For a moment, his eyes darkened, as if her words caught him off guard. But just as quickly, his lips moved in a faint smile. "Well, I can say one thing for, er, Jim. He sure has good taste." Then, as if his grin had been imagined, it faded, leaving only grimness. "I envy him," he added softly. It seemed as if he realized the situation he was in, and with this realization came a cold soberness.

Keeley didn't know how to respond to his statement or to him. His sudden change of moods made him more of an enigma to her than ever. An uncomfortable silence prevailed in the room with neither one wanting to break the spell. Each was lost in his own thoughts.

Linc, as he looked at Keeley, saw the uneasiness and the uncertainty that marred her beautiful features. She was a vision in a floral printed jersey dress that molded her lithesome figure to perfection in addition to emphasizing the golden flecks in her eyes. Her hair was swept away from her face, showing her finely boned features. Her ears, so delicately emphasized, were adorned with diamond stud earrings.

He had promised himself he would take her to dinner and talk business—nothing else, just business. When he had learned that his dream girl was none other than the owner's daughter, he had been consumed with rage. It had been a bitter pill to swallow, knowing that he had been duped. Then he had assured himself he didn't need the problems this woman would bring into his life. He needed all his faculties about him, because his one big dream in life was yet to be realized—the Super Bowl championship. He was determined to play football until he made that dream a reality. So, it would be better all the way around if he could forget who she was, what she looked like and the fact that he had ever touched her. And he would keep uppermost in his mind that she belonged to another man. His first priority was to get the best possible deal with the Timberjacks for the next year. And if it meant having dinner with the boss's daughter and discussing the contract, then so be it. He could handle that.

But when Keeley had flung open the door, he felt again the pull of her attraction. It wreaked the same havoc to his body as a whirlwind across the desert, forceful and destructive. Contract and good intentions became the furthest things from his mind. What he wanted to do instead was wrap his arms around her, hold her close, say to hell with convictions and forget that she could never be his for the taking. He found her utterly fascinating.

When the silence climbed to a silent scream, Keeley said bluntly, "Look, Mr. Hunter. Why don't we just forget about going to dinner, or anywhere else." She paused to open her purse and hastily withdrew a folded piece of paper. "Why don't we sit right here and discuss your contract. I have instructions from my father to listen to all your demands."

He sighed as he rubbed the back of his neck. "I think not," he replied coolly. "I've already made reservations for dinner."

She cocked her head to the left. "There's a phone on the bar. You can call and cancel them," she replied, equally as cool.

Linc looked at her, his face like stone, anger in every tense line of it. But his voice, when he spoke, belied his chaotic emotions.

"That's not what you want any more than I do." He moved closer and before she realized his intentions, a wandering hand reached out and began tracing the sweet curve of her jaw.

Suddenly her body was overheated. She tore her eyes away from him and took a panicky step backward. She felt as if they were circling, testing each other.

"How about if I offered an alternative suggestion," he said after a moment. The pitch of his voice had deepened to a husky level.

Keeley didn't trust him. She gave him a sidelong look, a frown puckering her eyebrows. "Wh—what?"

A flicker of a smile hovered around his mouth. "What if we call a truce for the evening and forget about talking business?" His eyes now held a twinkling gleam. "I don't think either one of us is in the right frame of mind to negotiate a contract. Do you?"

His words sent a jolt of incredulous shock through her. What did he mean, forget the contract? That was what it was all about, wasn't it? No business, no dinner. Wasn't that the deal? What could he have up his sleeve to warrant such a preposterous suggestion? Did he think that if he wined and dined and sweet-talked her now, she would later persuade her father to give him exactly what he wanted? Was the boss's daughter too much of a temptation to pass up? These questions kept seesawing through her mind until she felt dizzy.

"Keeley," he said, "can't you see that I don't give a damn about anything right now except being with you? Why is that so hard for you to understand?"

Keeley's tongue darted around her suddenly dry lips. "Linc, please. This—this is no good," she implored, shaking her head helplessly. "I'm engaged. I—you—" Her throat closed, making further speech impossible.

Linc sighed heavily as he rubbed the back of his neck. "Hell, don't you think I don't know that?" he exclaimed harshly. "I'm not exactly thrilled with my behavior either.'' He paused and looked down at her. ''But I still want to be with you anyway,'' he added in a somewhat strained voice.

Keeley felt as if she had run head on into a brick wall. This was all so crazy. Where was it all going to end? If they weren't going to discuss the contract, then there was absolutely no need to accept his invitation. But, heaven help her, she wanted to go with him! He aroused a sexual excitement in her that couldn't be denied. Since the first time she had laid eyes on him, something had happened to her. Every other man she had ever known, including her husband and fiancé, paled in comparison to Linc Hunter.

In making that admission, she was aware that she was flirting with danger. It was indeed a brazen and foolish thought. If she accepted his invitation, Linc was sure to think that she was interested in him. And her father would be absolutely livid if she went out to dinner and didn't discuss the contract. He hated failure in anyone—most of all his own daughter. Maybe in the end, however, her failure would work to her advantage by forcing Luther to let Stan or someone else on the staff handle future contract negotiations.

''Keeley?''

She felt her breath threaten to explode through her chest as she groped for the strength to say no, to tell him to go away and leave her alone. But the words wouldn't come. Once again her physical need overshadowed her sound judgment. She felt her heightened nerves slowly uncoil.

He had won.

''Linc,'' she began in a halting voice. ''I want you to know—'' He swiftly crossed the room and stood in front of her, causing her to stop in midsentence. He raised his hand as if to touch her lips, but then let it fall to his side.

"I understand," he said gently. "There's no need to say more."

Keeley nodded, not able to trust her voice. Her carefully attained equilibrium and common sense had been lost.

Reaching for the light jacket that lay on the couch, Linc draped it over her shoulders and, with a reassuring and gentle prod, guided her toward the door, his firm hand on her smooth elbow.

As the chilly night air kissed her skin, Keeley felt her befuddled senses return somewhat to normal. After being firmly planted in Linc's plush Cadillac Seville, she tried to relax while she waited for him to get in and start the engine. But she couldn't. Her heart was pounding recklessly with emotion.

Linc, sliding his large frame under the wheel, cast a searching glance in her direction, but she forced herself not to look at him. When his knee casually brushed her leg, she felt a burning sensation filter throughout her body. Quickly she stilled her features to show nothing of her emotional reaction.

There was no attempt to make small talk as they drove through the city and across the bridge that spanned the Columbia River. A short time later, Linc pulled into the parking lot of what looked to be an elegant but obscure restaurant. The raw smell of the river tickled her nose as he helped her out of the car and they made their way inside.

Keeley looked around the room, taking in its every detail. The candles at each table cast a warm glow over the entire area, giving it a relaxed and cozy atmosphere. Their table was next to a panel of glass that extended from floor to ceiling. As she peered out of it, she could see the twinkling lights of the tugboats as they moved the barges up and down the river. It was all quite peaceful and pleasant, and she was content to sit and watch the activities on this important waterway.

"Hey, did you forget about me?" Linc asked, his voice low and teasingly husky.

With a flush stealing up her cheeks, she halted her wandering eyes and turned around to face him. His eyes were resting knowingly on her.

"This is a lovely place," she remarked casually, then scolded herself for the odd catch she heard in her voice. She wanted desperately to break that sensual spell that had hovered over them since the moment she had opened her apartment door.

"But not nearly as lovely as you," he said in a deep, slow undertone. His eyes rested on her soft mouth before dropping to her breasts, so vividly nestled against the outline of her dress. He felt his muscles tighten and his tongue thicken as desire pounded through his body.

Keeley fought for oxygen as she turned swiftly away from his probing eyes.

Striving to put the conversation back on an even keel, Linc coughed and said, "I like it here, mainly because it's off the beaten track and none of Portland's rich and famous know about it." A boyish smile now teased one corner of his mouth.

"And you don't consider yourself to be in that category?" she asked lightly, relief at the change of conversation making her bold. She was also curious to know if everything she had heard about him was true.

His smile widened into a full grin. "Naughty, naughty, I fear your claws are showing, Mrs. Sanders. Remember our truce?"

A slight pink stained her cheeks at his gentle rap on the knuckles. Then she said rather stiffly, "Well, I know how most athletes love being in the public eye." She shrugged. "So I just assumed—"

His large hand reached over and clamped down on top of hers. This action halted her words in midsentence as nothing else could have done.

His eyes were now hard and piercing as they bore down into hers. "Don't ever make the mistake of comparing me with anyone else. Rest assured I've never sought the limelight, nor do I seek it now. Why do you think I chose this out-of-the-way spot? I'll tell you why! Because I like my privacy!"

Both the harsh words and the weight of his hand caused a shiver to pass through Keeley. He had certainly removed her claws in a hurry, she thought with building anger. But she was saved from trying to defend herself by the timely arrival of the waiter.

Withdrawing his hand, Linc turned around and greeted him with a smile.

Keeley was astounded at Linc's ability to turn burning anger into urbane politeness within a matter of seconds. In that moment she realized that he would be a dangerous adversary, for she could never be sure where she stood with him. She let out a labored breath as she studied his marblelike profile while he conversed with the waiter about wine. His nose, she decided, had definitely been broken. Every athlete she knew wore that particular mark of the trade. He was no exception. His chin jutted firm and strong—or maybe stubborn was a better word. A man who was used to having his way, she decided. And his eye-lashes... How could one best describe them?

"Keeley!" Linc's impatient voice canceled her daydreaming. "Is there a particular kind of wine you prefer?"

Keeley shook her head. "No—no. It doesn't matter. Anything you want will be fine with me."

She listened as Linc gave the order for a bottle of dry wine. She then turned her attention to the menu and pretended to study it. She felt his eyes on her, willing her to look at him, but she kept her head buried. She needed a moment away from his all-consuming eyes. Although he was every bit the macho athlete, she realized there was another side to him, a deeper sensitive side that set him apart from the others of his kind. He had proved that, hadn't he, by his reaction to her remark a moment ago?

"How about the chicken Cordon Bleu?"

The grating sound of his voice drew her head up abruptly. The waiter had reappeared and was looking at him, waiting.

"Oh, I'm—I'm sorry," she apologized. "That sounds good to me." Damn! She needed to get her act together! She was acting like a preschooler with a short attention span.

Linc nodded as the waiter poured a sip of wine into a glass for Linc to sample. Seeing he was satisfied, the waiter filled each of their glasses, then took the menus and left.

Linc, with a relaxed smile on his face, took a sip of his wine. "Now tell me a little about yourself," he insisted. "Do you work?"

"Of course I work," Keeley replied quickly and more sharply than she intended; but she wanted to set the record straight that she was no rich man's idle daughter living off her father's money.

He quirked an eyebrow and grinned. "I hate to say it again, but you're..."

"I know," she interrupted, a sheepish grin spreading across her lips. "I know, my claws are showing."

He chuckled warmly. "Well, maybe just a little, but I guess I can understand." His eyes became clouded. "Everything's happening so fast, it makes me feel a little funny, too."

The rich depth of his laughter and his blatant confession were a potent combination. They did strange things to her. She reached for her glass and took a rather large sip of wine. She needed something—anything—to help get her through the remainder of the evening.

"Hey, take it easy with that stuff," he advised gently. "It's not water, you know. Anyway, I want to at least hear your life story before you conk out on me."

This statement drew an impish smile from her, making the dimples in her cheeks deepen.

Suddenly, Linc wondered what it would feel like to delve his tongue into those tiny crevices and taste her soft creamy skin. He felt the blood literally pound through his body, leaving a fine line of perspiration above his lips. He shifted in his chair, striving to help ease the discomfort this tantalizing thought had brought to his body.

"Believe it or not," she was saying self-consciously, "my life story would only bore you."

The soft tone of Keeley's voice cut gently into his thoughts. "I doubt that," he said, bracing his forearms on the table and increasing the intensity of his gaze. "Nothing about you could ever bore me, Keeley Sanders—not even if I lived to be a doddering old man."

And he meant it too. Every word. But why? Why did she have such a profound effect on him? he wondered. It was more than her unique beauty, although he knew that that in itself would serve to turn many a man's head. Was it perhaps the loneliness that lurked in the depths of her eyes? It seemed to call to him. He wanted to forever touch her, protect her. In just two days he had become a driven man.

Keeley, stalling for time, took another sip of the tart liquid. She felt it rush immediately to her head. Her eyelashes fluttered shut for a moment. She wanted to blame her lightheadedness on the wine, but she couldn't, not when the driving force of Linc's masculinity surrounded her like a cocoon.

"Go on, tell me about your work," he insisted. "Don't be shy."

Keeley hesitated, running her fingers through her hair. "I teach early childhood classes at the university." She paused to drink the last sip of her wine and shook her head when Linc offered to refill her glass. She ignored his teasing grin and went on, "It's very rewarding thinking that you play a small part in shaping a child's mind."

He smiled. "It sounds very rewarding."

"Oh, it is," she responded with excitement dancing in her eyes. "But it also offers another advantage," she added.

He lifted his eyebrows. "And what is that?"

"Teaching in college enables me to spend more time with my father than if I were teaching in the public schools."

"Why is that so important?" he asked, sounding a trifle puzzled but sincere.

"Well, as you know, Luther's had several heart attacks and hasn't by any means recovered from the last one." She smiled. "It takes me, along with my aunt, to make him toe the line. He thinks he's much stronger than he actually is."

Linc laughed and rolled his eyes. "You don't have to tell me about Luther Cooper. I know him about as well as anyone. And I agree, he's about as bullheaded and stubborn as they come. You have my sympathy in trying to corral him."

She smiled back a bit grimly. "It's nice to know someone understands my plight."

"I take it the reason you have to spend so much time with him is because of his vast amount of business endeavors. Am I right?"

Her chin went up a fraction. "That's right. But how did you know?"

Linc shrugged. "Well, it's obvious he's turned over the reins of the Timberjacks to you—" He left the statement hanging, as if reluctant to go any further.

Keeley remained silent as she watched his large shapely fingers close around the wine bottle and pour himself another generous glass of the delicious liquid.

"Somehow I find it hard to believe that Luther would turn over the reins of the team's business to a woman, even if it is his own flesh and blood."

Keeley stared at him for a moment to see if he was serious and then, seeing that he was, lowered her lashes to hide her irritation. How dare he insinuate that she was some kind of lamebrained idiot who wasn't capable of undertaking what he obviously thought was a man's work? How chauvinistic! She was tempted to put him in his place once and for all. She probably had a better head for business than most men she knew. Just because she didn't want to negotiate contracts didn't mean she wasn't capable of it.

A look of confusion flittered across his face as he saw the way her features froze and her smile disappeared. "Did I say something wrong? I—"

"Oh, no," she said sarcastically, "you didn't say anything wrong. You just let me know exactly how you felt about women mixing in the world of sports." A blot of red stained each cheek.

"Hey, take it easy," he stressed hurriedly, his eyes dark with concern. "I'm sorry. I didn't mean that the way it sounded." Then on the heels of his apology he admitted reluctantly, "It was jealousy, pure and simple, that made me say it."

A puzzled frown creased her brow. "Jealousy? I don't understand," she stammered.

"Yes, jealousy. I don't want you ever talking or having anything to do with other members of the Timberjacks. Mine's not the only contract that's coming up for renewal, you know," he said by way of an explanation.

Keeley was flabbergasted and it showed. She opened her mouth to speak but then jammed her jaws back together when the words failed to pass through her lips.

Linc was staring at her now, his expression dark and brooding.

It was as if they were playing a game, waiting to see who would make the first move. How had their conversation gotten so completely out of hand? she wondered.

Suddenly, everything about him overwhelmed her—his aggressively handsome face, his smell, his driving personality, and his possessiveness. No doubt about it, this evening was a terrible mistake.

The waiter chose a most opportune moment to serve their dinner. As he placed the delicious chicken dish in front of her, Keeley felt her stomach turn upside down. Lowering her head, she made a pretense of straightening her napkin while breathing deeply, hoping to chase away the uneasy feeling.

When she finally raised her head, Linc said without pretense, "I apologize. Again. It seems as if nothing I've said or done this entire evening has been right." He grinned. "Apology seems to be the rule of thumb with me of late." He paused a moment. "Do you think we could start over? I promise not to open mouth and insert foot again. What d'you say?" A grin slashed across his mouth and his eyes twinkled mischievously.

When he looked at her that way, Keeley was powerless to deny him anything. She knew that admission would come to haunt her, but not now. At this moment, she was throwing sanity to the wind and giving in to the mounting pleasure that was now more potent than all the wine she had consumed.

But payday would surely come later.

During the remainder of the dinner they talked of many things: books, music, religion, films. Keeley realized during the course of the conversation that she knew absolutely nothing about his personal history. It suddenly rankled her that he knew far more about her than she did about him. She then found herself more curious than ever about what made him the way he was, what made him tick.

In the end, when she had despaired of ever learning anything about him, she decided to take matters into her own hands.

"Do you live, breathe and eat football as my father does?" she asked.

He grinned. "As a matter of fact I do. But somehow, methinks the lady disapproves."

She stiffened. "Not really. Everybody has to do their thing," she lied. How could he waste his life chasing rainbows? And that was exactly what he was doing, she thought. To her the game of football was nothing more than a sport—a sport that she felt wasn't intended to be a man's life work. Of course, she was prejudiced, but not unjustly so. Paul had done a good job of warping her mind against the sport itself as well as his fellow cohorts. He had seriously colored her judgment as far as athletes and athletics were concerned. She wanted as little to do with them as possible.

"Well, my 'thing,' as you so aptly phrased it, is most assuredly the contact sport. There's a challenge to be met that's equal to none other." He cocked his head back and narrowed his eyes. "You coming from an avid sports-minded father, I find it hard to believe you hold such scorn for the sport. Is there a reason?"

The tension was almost tangible, now, as it leapt between them. She looked closely at his face for clues as to how much he actually knew about her background. For some reason, she felt he knew everything. He was the type that once he had learned who she was, he'd leave no stone unturned until he had uncovered every single detail about her.

Suddenly she became aware of a throb behind her temple. "My—my husband was a football player turned coach. I found out the hard way that I wasn't cut out for that kind of life."

A strained silence followed her words.

"How long were you married?" Linc asked, breaking into the unnerving quiet.

"Two miserable years," she answered with feeling.

"I'm sorry."

Keeley dug her nails into her palms. "Don't be. I've long passed that point myself. Our marriage was doomed from the start."

"Care to tell me about it?" he asked casually. His tone was soft.

Keeley was finding it difficult to swallow. "I—I married Paul right out of college without my—my father's blessings."

Linc frowned. "And that caused your marriage to fail?"

"No, no, of course not. I would never transfer the blame to my father's shoulders." She paused to lick her hot, dry lips. It was hard, even now, to talk about her past. "Luther thought I could do much better than marry a coach. He knew the kind of life players and coaches are forced to lead, and he wanted a better life for me." Another pause. "I don't think he ever forgave me for marrying against his wishes. He never liked Paul and made no effort to hide it."

"I take it Luther was right?" Linc pressed, encouraging her to keep talking.

Keeley sighed audibly. "Partly. It wasn't so much the way I was forced to live—although I didn't particularly like it, I could have endured it. No, it was Paul's and my personality. We just didn't click." A flicker of pain crossed her eyes. "He constantly craved excitement, which to him was parties and drinking. Next to coaching, they were more important than anything else.''

"Then he was a damn fool," Linc said quietly.

Keeley took a sip of water, hoping to hide the flush his words brought to her cheeks. "I kept hoping things would change for the better, but they never did.''

"Go on," Linc urged.

Keeley suddenly shook her head. "No, please—I can't. I've—I've talked too much already." What in the world had possessed her to confess so freely and blatantly her innermost heartbreak and secrets? She was appalled. Surely it had to be the amount of wine she had consumed that had loosened her tongue so.

"You've already gone this far," he urged huskily. "Please don't quit now."

She averted her eyes, suddenly embarrassed. "No—really, Linc. I've already said far too much."

"Would it make any difference," he countered softly, "if I told you I'm not being just curious, but that I'm genuinely interested in knowing everything there is to know about you?" The tone of his voice was low-key and soothing, but nevertheless pressing.

When she swung back around to face him, a gentle sweetness was pouring from his eyes, giving her courage.

She pushed aside the lump in her throat and continued, "Although Paul wasn't interested in having a family, I thought it would strengthen our marriage. I wanted desperately to make it work. So I took matters into my own hands and finagled it so that I became pregnant.''

"And?" Linc encouraged, sensing once again she wasn't going to continue unless prodded.

Keeley drew a long shuddering breath. "We attended a party one evening and Paul got drunk. On the way home, we were involved in a collision." She paused to lick her parched lips. "The accident took Paul's life and that of our unborn child. In addition my father suffered his first heart attack," she added in a flat, listless voice. Even now she could still hear the squeal of tires, the scrape of metal, her and Paul's mingled cries, the smell of burning rubber.... She closed her eyes against the blinding pain of remembering.

Linc's sharp intake of breath echoed around the quiet room.

Then as if driven by an unknown demon she went on, "For a while I nearly went crazy. I wanted to die, too. And during this time my father was another cross I had to bear. He was so devastated over the loss of the baby that his recovery was slow. Then when he did improve, he began to smother me with unwanted sympathy."

Suddenly Linc's hand snaked out and closed around hers, claiming her voice for a moment. Her heart galloped as his fingers meshed with hers in understanding.

"So what happened then?" he encouraged softly.

Keeley had difficulty getting her mind back on track. "When—when I refused to let him coddle me and take over my life again, he started to rehash accusations about my having married Paul." She paused and cleared her throat. "From there our relationship went from bad to worse. I left Portland and went back to Eugene and began teaching at the college. That's where I met Jim. Thanks to his help and understanding, I was finally able to put my life back together." She threw her head back defiantly. "Now I'm looking forward to our future together."

"I wouldn't be too sure of that if I were you," Linc stressed evenly, although a vein twitching in his neck belied his calmness.

"Well, I'm sure of it." She lashed back at him. "Pain and disillusionment are hard teachers. Once you've been burned, you don't go back for more." She had said it. She had let him know in simple terms that his pursuit of her—if that was what one could call it—was all in vain.

She refused to let Linc Hunter threaten the security of her life. She had everything mapped out according to plan. She would marry Jim, have a couple of bright-eyed children and fill their home with love and laughter. There simply wasn't room in her life for the likes of Linc Hunter.

"That seems to be the consensus among many athletes' and coaches' wives," he stated, breaking into her turbulent thoughts. His voice held strong bitterness.

It was Keeley's turn to look at him with questioning eyes, though she remained quiet, making an effort to shelve once again her own painful past.

Shortly he spoke, his tone still laced with bitterness. "My brother was another prime example of a perfect mismatch."

"Was?"

His full lower lip thinned into a white line. "You heard right." He then sighed heavily as he pushed his empty plate aside. "My younger brother was twenty-two years old and facing a brilliant career in the N.F.L. when he lost his life in a boating accident.''

Sympathy pinched Keeley's features. "Oh, I'm— I'm sorry. I—"

Linc reached over and quickly squeezed her hand, halting her words.

Then, withdrawing his hand, he continued, "My brother came home one morning following a road game and found a note from his 'socialite' wife. It stated that marriage to a roughneck football player could no longer be endured. The bright lights and culture of New York City were calling to her." His voice was now filled with both contempt and pain. "They were living at the time in Dallas, Texas, where Joe was a rookie for the Dallas Cowboys. After reading the letter, he immediately took his boat to a nearby lake, and two days later they found his body washed up on the bank." He paused and blinked. "It reminds me very much of your tragedy. So damned senseless."

Keeley felt sick. "I—I agree," she whispered.

He went on as if she hadn't spoken. "If I could have gotten my hands on his wife at the time, I would've killed her with my bare hands. I swear it!"

The pain in his eyes had been replaced by a cold hardness, and a muscle twitched in his jaw. There was no doubt he meant every word he said.

Keeley shivered and wrapped her arms around her chest as if to ward off the coolness that was shooting from his eyes. "Are—are you positive he took his own life?"

He grimaced. "I knew my brother well and that little bitch—" He broke off abruptly, remembering to whom he was talking. "Anyway," he added, "she had him wrapped around her little finger, and if she'd asked him to quit football, the foolish kid would've done it.''

Keeley kept silent this time. What more could she say that hadn't already been said? She toyed with her food until the silence lengthened and became almost deafening. Then, following Linc, she laid down her fork and pushed her plate away. Food was the furthest thing from her mind.

The waiter appeared and instantly whisked away their plates. He suggested a dessert which they both turned down. Keeley asked for coffee instead, as did Linc.

After the coffee was served, Linc said, ''I hope the torrid rehashing of my past wasn't too much for you on top of forcing you to rake up your old hurts.'' His piercing gaze centered on her face. ''It certainly made me realize, though, how much more you lost than I did.''

Keeley accepted his last comment for what it was and let it pass unanswered. ''Somehow I think you missed your calling,'' she replied instead.

''Oh, how is that?''

She smiled, relaxing a little. ''The way you gave me the third degree, you would've made a good lawyer.''

A half-smile tugged at the corners of his mouth. ''And *I* think you would've made a good psychiatrist.''

''Oh?'' She grinned openly.

''You're such a good listener. Not everyone has that quality.'' His eyes were again warm and melting as they moved over her face.

She lowered her eyes, an embarrassed sting flushing her cheeks. "If I didn't know better, I'd say we were forming a mutual admiration society."

He laughed out loud. "Sounds like a great idea to me."

This silliness has gone far enough, she thought. She quickly tried to divert his attention by asking, "Was your brother your only family?"

But she didn't fool him. There was a teasing glint in his eyes as he replied, "No, both my parents are alive and well. For which I'm thankful," he added lightly. "They live in Pendleton, close to the Blue Mountains, where my dad dabbles in sheep farming, when he's not following me around the country, that is. He seems to think I can't play a game unless he's there. I don't know how much longer he can keep up the pace."

Keeley noticed that there was a satisfied ease about him when he spoke about his parents. She recognized immediately that there was a special bond between them. She imagined that he had borne the brunt of his parents' pain and grief throughout the whole ordeal of his brother's death as well as during the intervening years. For a moment, she envied Linc his doting parents and warm home life.

"Keeley, are you about ready to get out of here?" His soft tone cut gently into her thoughts.

A quiver of pleasure skipped through her veins at the husky way he spoke her name. When she turned to face him, however, he was signing the ticket the waiter had stuck in front of him. Without warning, perspiration dampened her palms. Now that the dinner was actually over and no contract had been discussed, she felt a panicky feeling replace the sense of pleasure.

Keeley shuddered to think what her father and Jim would do if they were to find out about this cozy dinner for two. Before tomorrow morning she had to come up with something to appease her father. Admitting that she hadn't even discussed Linc's contract was out of the question; it was entirely too risky. Suddenly the burden of guilt and deceit turned her stomach sour; it was almost too heavy to bear.

The night air had grown quite chilly, Keeley noticed as she stood next to Linc waiting for the car to be brought around to them. His hand remained firmly planted around her arm, so that every time she made even the slightest move, she brushed against his length.

What now? she wondered. Would Linc deposit her at the door of her apartment and walk out of her life? That was what she wanted, wasn't it? Never to see him again except maybe through a pair of binoculars as she watched him perform on the football field? Why, then, was her heart filled with a nameless longing as she gave him a sidelong glance?

She sensed that he too was holding himself in check as if the sensuous rub of their bodies was having an equally potent effect on him. His eyes smoldered as he saw her safely into the car before slamming the door and briskly walking around to ease himself behind the wheel.

Emotion ricocheted between them as they passed through the vacant streets of Portland. Keeley practically held her breath the entire way to her apartment, afraid to speak, afraid to move, for fear of triggering that unknown bomb that hovered over them, needing only the slightest excuse to erupt and blow her structured life to smithereens.

Only when he pulled up next to the curb in front of her door did she feel a little more at ease and secure. It was nearly all over now, and she had survived without making a fool of herself. For that much she could be thankful, she told herself as she firmly closed her hand around the door handle ready to spring from the car.

But she hadn't counted on Linc's agility. His hand, swift and sure, reached over and clamped down on her shoulder, holding her in a viselike grip. At first she tried to pull away, fright squeezing her insides, but then, against her will, she let her body be drawn against him. The contact with his hard, sinewy body caused a warm rush of response to flow through her.

"Keeley—oh, God," he began, only to have his words stifled against the sweet contours of her mouth. With the hungry touch of his lips to hers, Keeley was no longer in control of the situation. She felt herself drowning in the mastery of his questing mouth. She prayed for the sweet torture to never end.

Perhaps it was the knowledge that she was tasting forbidden fruit that added to the excitement of his touch. As the ardor of his kiss increased, so did the pressure to her fragile bones.

Keeley moaned against the now demanding force of his mouth as she struggled to get into a more comfortable position. His hold became instantly gentle as he sensed she was no longer trying to resist or escape him.

His tongue became a gentle invader as it swept with plundering thoroughness throughout her honeyed mouth. Keeley found herself sinking into quicksand so deep that it threatened to pull her under.

When he finally withdrew his mouth, she felt cheated.

"Oh, Keeley, tell me this isn't a dream," Linc begged huskily before easing his tongue into the fragile center of her ear.

She froze as a warmness so hot and intense spread to the very center of her being. She felt his hand move upward and begin kneading her breasts, not hurtfully, but lovingly, as though she were a delicate piece of porcelain that would crumble if not handled with tender care.

For a big man, whose hands and body were strong as well as sometimes brutal in carrying out the duties of his chosen profession, he had a most tender touch. She felt her nipples answer his questing fingers with a will all their own. They hardened and wanted so desperately to break through the confining garments and feel skin against skin.

Judging from Linc's ragged breathing and the coiled tightness of his muscles underneath her hand, Keeley sensed that he craved more, so much more than he was taking. Although with that insight came the knowledge that he would never demand of her more than she was willing to give. She need never fear him. Suddenly, it dawned on her that Linc was letting her set the pace. Wherever she led, he would follow.

It was that profound revelation that served to arouse her from the drugged power of Linc's hot mouth and hands.

She was allowing this man, a stranger, freedoms with her body that she had never allowed Jim. Jim. As his name flew to the surface of her mind, so did shame, as she realized the danger of what she was doing to herself and to him.

She was jeopardizing everything that was important to her, everything that made life worthwhile, for a moment's pleasure in the arms of a stranger. Didn't her past count for something?

Linc, sensing she was no longer a willing partner, lifted his head and stared at her with a puzzled look in his still-glazed eyes. She could see them shining from the glow of the streetlight.

"Keeley—?"

His voice told her he was in pain.

"Please," he groaned, "can we go into your apartment?"

For a fleeting instant, Keeley was tempted to give in to the torn pleading in his voice, in spite of the dressing down she had just given herself. She ached—ached for his touch.

When Linc's mouth sought hers a second time, with more urgency than before, the danger signals struck her brain like a jagged bolt of lightning.

"No!" She shook her head fiercely as she withdrew her lips. She then moved as far away from him as the seating arrangement would allow. She sucked in her breath, trying to drown out the quiver that shook her voice. "This is wrong! You're seeing a side of me that I didn't know existed." She paused to gulp back the tears crowding her eyes. "Please, just leave me alone!" she added on a last desperate note.

Before Linc realized her intentions, Keeley had the door open and was out of the car. Without a backward glance, she bolted up the steps and into her apartment.

Linc's "Damn it, Keeley, come back here!" fell on deaf ears as the sound of the closing door screamed loudly in the silent night air.

Four

How long Linc sat slumped down in the seat with his head slung back, he didn't know. His mind was so muddled and his body so battered that he felt as if he'd just stepped off the gridiron from playing the hard-hitting Pittsburgh Steelers. In fact, playing the Steelers would have been preferable to the beating his body had taken at Keeley's hands. The entire bittersweet episode had been his fault; the blame rested on his shoulders. He had allowed things to go too far.

His first thought after Keeley had dashed from the car like a scared deer was to follow her, knock down the door if necessary and try to make her listen to reason. But instinct told him that to crowd her now would be a fatal mistake. It would do irreparable damage. And what could he have said, anyway? That he was sorry for sampling something that belonged to another man?

Instead he had buried his face in his hands and remained glued to the seat with his tormented thoughts and a pounding head as his only companions. He could remember but one other time in his life when he had felt or been so frustrated with a situation. And that was when his brother was found dead. Then only his mind had been affected, not his body.

Linc didn't move. Thoughts of Keeley held him trapped. What was there about her that affected him in such a way? He felt both violent and tender as he conjured up in his mind's eye the fullness of her breasts and the pebble-hardness of her nipples that had leapt at his touch even through the material of her dress; the passion-drenched beauty of her face and the clean, sweet smell of her hair as he had buried his face in it. He felt a disturbing need to find out what was drawing him to her before it drove him crazy.

Just thinking about it caused perspiration to form above his eyebrows and above his lips. His hands were clenched around the steering wheel so hard he felt them become numb from poor circulation.

"Damn!" he cursed aloud. This kind of thinking is no good! he told himself. What he needed now more than anything was a good stiff drink. With his face contorted into a brooding knot of anger, he cranked the car, jerked the gear into drive and spun off into the inky blackness.

The moment Keeley reached the safety of her apartment, she immediately locked and chained the door and then waited with the sound of her own noisy heartbeat to see if Linc would follow. When nothing happened after several minutes of standing immobile, she crossed the room to the table lamp and switched it on. A dull glow saturated the room.

Biting down on her lower lip to stop its trembling, Keeley moved to the nearest front window and very slowly drew the curtain aside just enough so that she had a clear view of the street. She bit down on her lip harder, tasting the blood this punishment drew. It was as she had feared, Linc's car had not moved. The Seville loomed larger than ever on the dark and lonely street.

Her thoughts began darting in several different directions all at once, consumed with guilt and paranoia. How could she live with herself after tonight? she taunted helplessly. What had Linc said about all this being a dream? She wished with all her heart it had been just a dream. How could she possibly look Jim in the face after the way she had behaved?

Angela was right, she acknowledged now with stabbing honesty. Linc Hunter had indeed put a hex on her. At the time she had scoffed at her friend's prediction, but now it had come to haunt her. True, she was a grown woman, who had been married, with all the needs of any woman fitting into that category. But to practically throw herself into Linc's arms and allow him such liberties was unthinkable. She was definitely not a sex-starved widow. If she had been, Jim would have been more than willing to oblige her.

But she had kept Jim at arm's length all these months, telling herself and him that she needed more time to adjust to the physical side of their commitment. Her first marriage had taught her many things, but fulfillment in bed was not one of them. Paul couldn't have cared less if she enjoyed sharing his bed or not. He merely took from her and never gave in return.

Tonight, in the arms of Linc Hunter, she had experienced more enjoyment and fulfillment than all the times put together she had lain in her husband's arms. Lack of common interests hadn't been the only disastrous factor in their marriage.

She wondered now if Linc's thoughts were as painful as hers as he remained closeted in his car with the gloomy shadows of night dancing around him. What was he thinking? Was he feeling sick that he had fallen short of getting the boss's daughter into the sack? She felt the blood in her veins turn to ice water just thinking about how close she had come to letting that happen.

"How could you, Keeley Sanders!" she muttered aloud, with all the pent-up hostility she could muster. "How could you!"

She remained motionless and watched while the salty tears, one by one, trickled slowly down her cheeks and into her mouth.

Keeley, much to her father's disgust, put in many extra hours at the university during the next week. After a long talk with Judith, she had been able to pull herself together and plunge headfirst into the work she had neglected. Luther was getting along so well that she felt she could be away from him for several days. Anyway, it was imperative to Keeley's peace of mind that she remain out of his reach until he had time to cool off from what he saw as a botched-up job on her part in dealing with Linc.

On Sunday when she had returned to her apartment following a long heart-to-heart with Judith, the phone was ringing off the wall. Of course, it had been Luther, although for a heart-stopping moment she had feared it might be Linc. Her father had demanded an immediate accounting of where she had been for the last two hours, plus he had wanted to know, down to the last detail, everything that was discussed between her and Linc.

By some quirk of luck, she had managed to convince him that Linc was not as ready to discuss his contract as his agent had led Luther to believe. That statement had drawn a string of curse words followed by a sworn promise to make Linc's agent, first thing Monday morning, either put up or shut up. Though not entirely fair to her father, it had served to take the heat off her. Since he had learned about the break-down in negotiations, he had failed to ask any further questions concerning the evening. Although she knew the battle with her father was far from over, it had been temporarily shelved.

Now, as she sat at her desk, poring over sets of ungraded papers, it was Linc's face that kept staring up at her from the page instead of the words that her students had so carefully placed there. Why couldn't she forget him? Forget the feel of his hard, muscular body that had responded to her touch like lilies to spring water? Forget the way his mouth had drawn the nectar from hers as if he depended upon it for nourishment? Forget the way he had drawn her close to his heart and in one brief interlude taught her the true joy of touching and giving in tenderness? Forget? Impossible! To forget would be to stop breathing.

Although she had promised Judith she would put the encounter with Linc behind her, she found she could not. His image continued to haunt her relent-lessly, along with the ever-present guilt. Today was no different.

Keeley breathed a sigh of relief as the shrill ring of the phone beside her jerked her back to reality. She no longer lived in fright of picking up the instrument; she was positive now that Linc had no intention of getting in touch with her. Why should he? He didn't have to beg for his favors. There were plenty of women who would be more than willing to fall into bed with the great Linc Hunter. He didn't need her. And he certainly didn't need to worry about a place on a roster either; every team in the league would like to sign Linc Hunter.

"Hello," she said at last, her voice sounding like she was down in a well.

"Keeley?"

"Oh, hi, Dad. Yes, it's me." She could tell that he hadn't recognized her voice.

"Well, for a minute there, girl, you didn't sound like yourself. What's the matter, you got a cold?"

Keeley tapped her pencil against the desk. "No, I don't have a cold. I was just buried in grading papers, that's all," she lied.

"Hell, you've been working too hard all week. It's pretty bad when you don't even have time to visit your sick old man!"

This drew a smile from Keeley. "Dad," she said with controlled patience, "if I didn't know better, I'd think you were feeling a little sorry for yourself."

"You're mighty right I am!" he replied gruffly. "Nothing or nobody is cooperating with me. I haven't been able to get hold of Linc's agent on the phone. Nor have I had any luck talking to Linc personally. He's managed to escape me at every turn."

At the mention of Linc's name, Keeley felt her heart turn over.

"Dad, if you'll just be patient, I'm sure Stan—"

"Stan, hell! I've already told you I don't want Stan—"

"I know," Keeley cut in, "you don't want Stan messing in your business." She sighed and chewed on her lower lip in frustration. Guilt was ripping her

heart to pieces. But she couldn't let Luther's plead-
ings make her agree to see Linc again. She knew how
important it was to her father, but she owed it to herself and to Jim to remain firm—even at the risk of
hurting Luther. "Please, Dad, if you don't mind, let's
not discuss this again, not now anyway. Perhaps, if
you continue to improve, you can get Linc's name on
the document yourself."

"All right, girl," he said disgustedly. "I'll be quiet
for now, but I'm not about to let you off the hook. I
still intend for you to take charge of *all* my business
affairs, so don't think you can placate me by painting
rosy pictures about my health. I know the score," he
added, his voice sounding tired and dejected.

Keeley felt pain and remorse shoot through her
body like adrenaline. The glowing reports she had
received the past few days from Judith concerning her
father's health had made her temporarily blind to the
fact that he was still very ill. Although he was better,
she must keep in mind that he had a long way to go
before he could be considered a *well* man.

"Keeley, you still there?"

"Yes, Dad, I'm still here." She tried to inject a
note of brightness in her voice, hoping to ease the
tension between them.

"Good. Now about why I called." His voice, too,
sounded lighter, more cheerful. "I want you to go to
the game with me tonight." Ignoring her startled intake of breath that vibrated through the line, he went
on, "It's the last preseason game, and I insist that you
go. Anyway," he added petulantly, "Judith has some
confounded meeting at the school tonight she wants
to attend; although she said she would miss it if I

insisted.'' He paused. ''But I assured her that you had agreed to go with me.''

Keeley clutched the pencil in her hand so tightly that it snapped in two. To go to the game would mean seeing Linc, and she couldn't face that—not now. It was too soon—much too soon.

''Keeley, please.'' His voice held a pleading note that she was unused to hearing in her father's voice. He knew it would be a battle to get her to attend the game, so he was using his most powerful force to try and convince her—sympathy. He was playing that emotion to the hilt.

And just a few days ago it would have worked like magic. But then, she hadn't met Linc; hadn't known his passionate embrace; hadn't known the hungry quest of his lips and hands.

For a crazy moment, she was tempted to slam down the receiver and run away from it all. But she couldn't do that. Luther would never forgive her, nor would she ever forgive herself for acting so childish.

''No. I can't go,'' she finally managed to get out, though her throat had to work overtime just to allow her to say that much.

There was a moment of painful silence before Luther said hoarsely, ''All right. Have it your own way. I won't beg you, girl. For no matter what you may think, I understand. I may be a fool, but I'm not an insensitive fool!''

The line went dead with a soft click.

Keeley remained in a puzzled stupor for a few seconds with the telephone receiver suspended in midair. What on earth had Luther meant? Then it hit her forcefully between the eyes that he was referring to all the pain that Paul had put her through. He thought that because of it, she simply couldn't bear to attend any more games. At one time his assumption would have been true. But not now. It wasn't the past rearing its ugly head, but the present that was the serpent in her garden of Eden. It wasn't attending the game itself that caused her heart to palpitate, but the thought of seeing Linc. Football and Linc Hunter were now synonymous.

How could she be so callous and selfish in letting Luther think she was still haunted by the past? It wasn't fair, she argued. But she couldn't let him know about her present dilemma either. Was it possible that she could attend the game and block out the fact that Linc was on the field—pretend he didn't exist? It was a matter of putting things in their right perspective, she told herself objectively. She had made a decision to put Linc out of her life. Now she must jump the next hurdle.

After all, didn't she have a promised responsibility to her father to help him with the team's business? If she didn't want him to get suspicious, she had to get her act together and gain control of her emotions.

With shaking fingers and halting breath, Keeley lifted the receiver and dialed her father's number. It rang several times before she heard his gruff voice say hello.

"Dad, I've changed my mind."

As they traveled to the stadium Keeley concentrated on the smell of fall that permeated the air. Its crisp freshness infiltrated the close confines of the car's interior, bringing to mind that this was her favorite time of the year. Purposefully, she stared out the window at the trees. They were absolutely gorgeous as they stood robed in their leaves of brilliant colors. September always made the first visible change in the foliage, and this year was no exception. In the early evening twilight, the burnt oranges, the crimsons, the golds, were splashed together creating a masterpiece that no artist with his brush could equal.

As Keeley accompanied her father into the lower level of the massive dome stadium, Linc's sunny smile and twinkling eyes suddenly flashed before her mind's eye. In some ways it was hard for her to believe that he was a part of this rough sport. She was well aware that he was a competitor—he had made that quite plain to her—but there was also a gentle side to him that didn't seem compatible with this hard-hitting revelry. The thought of him seeking vengeance on the field as the pursuer or the pursued caused a momentary tightening around her heart.

Forcing these unsettling and forbidden thoughts aside, Keeley instead concentrated on helping her father get comfortable in his box seat. As the controlling owner of the highly prestigious Portland Timberjacks, Luther Cooper had the best seats available. Besides Keeley, there were several aides always waiting in the shadows to do his bidding. He was too absorbed with what was happening around him to notice or to care. He was so excited about being able to attend the game that he was like a small child with a new toy. Keeley smiled to herself as she sat back and watched as he took in the festivities around him.

This last preseason game between the Timberjacks and the Houston Oilers was expected to be a hot one. As the time drew near for the regular season games to begin, the rivalry became more intense.

"Well, are you glad you came?"

Luther's excited voice brought Keeley back sharply to the moment at hand. Turning toward him, she smiled sweetly and said, "I didn't realize that I'd actually missed all this until now." She leaned over and sealed her admission with a quick kiss. "I'm glad you twisted my arm and made me come." And she meant it too. Now that she was here, she was determined to stick to her resolutions concerning Linc and really enjoy the evening.

"Huh!" Luther said as he drew back in mock horror, though a pleased smile lifted the corners of his lips. "Twisting your arm is an understatement. Browbeating and threatening are much closer to the truth."

Keeley flushed. "Well, I'm here now, so I hope you're satisfied." A smile took the edge off her words.

"I'm satisfied all right; although it would be nice if Judith were here with us." He shook his head. "Can't understand how a damned meeting could be more important than watching this clash between the Timberjacks and the Oilers. I'll never understand it."

Keeley turned her head to hide the grin that covered her face. Luther had never accepted the fact that the women in his life didn't enjoy sports as much as he did. It was an obsession with him, so it should be with them as well. Keeley couldn't wait to tell Judith what Luther had said. It would draw a hearty chuckle from her.

Also, Keeley sensed that her father missed Judith. They were coming to depend on each other more and more, though she dared not hope anything would ever come of it, for fear of disappointment. But just the same, the thought formed a warm glow around her heart.

"Speaking of absenteeism, where's Stan?" Keeley asked. "I would've sworn wild horses couldn't have kept him away from this game."

A devilish grin spread slowly across Luther's face. "Well, a wild horse did just that. Millie dragged him off to Florida."

"Florida!"

"Yup. You heard me right. Carolyn, their oldest daughter, went into labor with her first child yesterday, and Millie insisted that Stan go with her."

Keeley grinned and shook her head. "Poor Stan."

"Don't 'poor Stan' me," Luther mimicked roughly. "They deserve one another, if you ask me."

A frown weaved its way between Keeley's brows. "Don't you think it's about time you and Stan settled your differences?"

"Not until he gets off my back about the way I run the team. He's a constant thorn in my side."

With a pensive sigh Keeley let the subject die. There was no point in adding fuel to the fire, she decided. When the Timberjacks began to show a profit, she felt sure that tempers would cool down and old friendships would prevail.

Then a sudden burst of cheering and yelling claimed her attention. She snapped her head back toward the field. The lighted screen in the middle of the stadium was flashing encouraging words to the Timberjacks. This served to draw a rousing response from the capacity crowd. The maroon and white pompoms were bouncing up and down in time to the music provided by several area bands. Many of the fans were already standing and shouting in anticipation of the starting whistle.

"Damn!" Luther exclaimed excitedly. "Have you

ever seen anything like these fans? By the way they're responding, you'd think we were playing for the division championship. This is definitely going to be our year. I can feel it in these creepy old bones," he finished with fire in his eyes.

"Shhh," she cautioned in a soothing voice and patted him on the arm. "I want you to enjoy yourself, but remember the doctor said no cheering or foot stomping, or getting too excited. After all, this is only an exhibition game."

Luther jerked his head around. "Girl, when are you going to learn that there isn't such a thing as just an exhibition game. Every game counts as far as I'm concerned. And I expect my players to perform that way every time they hit the field."

Keeley laughed. "You've made your point, Dad. My lips are sealed forever on the subject."

"Good."

This drew another laugh from Keeley before the spectators once more claimed her attention.

The crowd, on its feet now, rocked the building with boos as the Houston Oilers took the field. Oh, God. Keeley winced, aware that soon she would see Linc again.

With legs threatening to buckle beneath her, Keeley stood alongside her father, careful not to let her turbulent emotions show, and watched as the Timberjacks surged onto the artificial turf. The boos turned instantly to cheers. Then without hesitation or apology, Keeley's eyes immediately searched the players that dotted the sidelines until she spotted a particular crown of sandy hair, wearing number twelve. There her gaze rested for a lengthy moment.

The noise of the crowd, led by the Ladyjack cheerleaders, had risen to a thundering roar, but Keeley was oblivious to all except the actions of a certain number twelve. She found herself following his every move.

Suddenly, she realized what she was doing and quickly averted her eyes. She felt hysteria begin to bubble just behind her composed facade. She gripped her clammy hands tightly together, completely ignoring the pain this action brought.

How could she break the promise to herself to keep thoughts of Linc Hunter at bay? Why was she destroying herself like this? She was being given a second chance to have a stable home and a family life with Jim.

How dare she put it all in jeopardy by her continued obsession for a man who so obviously didn't return her feelings?

Keeley had felt a surge of relief wash over her when the winning field goal was kicked by the Timberjacks and the game ended. Then, as if pulled by a magnet and adding punishment to shame, she had turned and watched Linc, looking extremely weary and hunched-shouldered, leave the field.

Now as the Cadillac neared her apartment, she felt a different type of relief overtake her. She would soon be in the privacy of her own home, away from football *and* Linc Hunter. However, her father's next words indicated an unexpected setback to her plans.

"With each passing day," Luther stated emphatically, "our chance of losing Linc Hunter increases. He's a dynamite quarterback as well as a team leader. We must, and I underline *must*, reach a contractual agreement with him." The corners of his mouth turned downward. "The other stockholders are getting mighty edgy, too."

"Dad, please—" Keeley pleaded. She squelched the urge to cover her ears with her hands.

"Don't interrupt, let me finish," he said brusquely. "Since the doctor let me go to the game tonight, I'm hoping he'll let me spend a few hours a day at the office." He paused and smote a fist in his hand. "I'm determined—"

"No!" Keeley broke in heatedly. "It's much too soon for you to even be thinking along those lines." A deep frown marred her smooth brow. "Besides, Dr. Willis told you it may be six more months before you could do any type of strenuous work."

Keeley barely noticed that they were now parked in front of her apartment. She was too upset over Luther's stubbornness. It was an impossibility, his returning to the office for even an hour a day. His job was entirely too demanding for a well man, much less one who had been gravely ill.

"Well, then, are you willing to meet with Linc or his agent or both and give it another try?"

Keeley felt as if the solid ground had been ripped from beneath her feet. She bit back the stifled cry that threatened to erupt from her lips as her mind became flooded with waves of mixed emotions and questions. Had Luther intentionally used his work *and* Linc in order to get her to take part in the negotiations again? Or was he sincere in thinking that he was really going to lose his ace quarterback at the end of the year and was just desperate enough to use any means available to him to keep it from happening?

Although she hadn't come right out and said as much, Luther knew she had no further plans to meet with Linc. There had to be another way for her father to get a commitment from Linc other than through her. *There just had to be!* She didn't know how much longer she could handle the burden of guilt that gnawed constantly at her insides.

But right now, she was too weary to delve for the answers to these questions. And judging from the drawn look on Luther's features, he felt the same way.

Keeley *wasn't* too tired to know that she had no intention of seeing Linc again—for any reason.

Luther's head now lay back against the cushioned seat. His eyes were closed. Peering at him closely, she realized with a pang that while he was waiting for her answer he had fallen asleep. As the light from the street lamp flickered across his face, she noted how worn out and old he looked.

With tears pricking her eyes, she leaned over and kissed him gently on the cheek before signaling to John that she was ready to go. It was with a heavy heart that she made her way up the steps and into her silent apartment.

Keeley had just drawn back the sheet and was preparing to crawl into bed when the doorbell rang. For a startled moment, she thought her ears were playing tricks on her; then she heard it again, this time more insistent.

Grabbing a light flannel robe from her closet, she hurriedly threw her arms into it as she made her way into the living room. Pausing, she reached for the switch on the table lamp. After realizing that it was indeed the doorbell, her first and foremost thought was of Luther. Something had happened to him!

With pounding heart and clammy hands, Keeley

remained motionless in front of the door for one paralyzed moment. Although she placed her hand on the knob, she didn't turn it. She was afraid.

"Who—who's there?"

Silence.

"Please! Who's there?" Keeley repeated, her voice scarcely above a whisper.

"Linc."

"Linc?" she repeated dumbly.

"Yes, Linc."

Keeley wet her lips nervously. "What—what do you want?"

"Keeley, please, open the door." His voice sounded muffled.

The entire time her hands fumbled with the deadbolt lock, an inner voice warned: *Don't do this, you'll be sorry. Don't do this!* With hands that seemed to be disjointed from her body, Keeley slowly drew open the door. Linc Hunter, dressed casually in a knit shirt and jogging pants, crossed the threshold very slowly and walked to the middle of the room.

Keeley quietly closed the door and leaned weakly against it. She stared at him, trembling.

"I guess you're wondering why I'm here," he said at length, his voice ragged.

Keeley swallowed hard, but still no words escaped her lips. She was not only shocked to see him, but she was doubly shocked at his appearance. He looked exactly like he had been in a boxing match and lost. He was bruised, battered and beat up. She was certainly correct in thinking he'd been abused on the field this evening. What a high price to pay, she thought bitterly, for a moment's glory on the gridiron. If only he hadn't come to her door and let her see

him like this. She mustn't let his condition weaken
her resolve not to deal with him anymore.

Suddenly she felt her stomach plummet to her toes.
Why indeed had he come to her door at this time of
night? She hadn't seen or heard from him in over a
week—not that she wanted to, she told herself
quickly. But why was he here now? Was he looking
for sympathy, or something else? she wondered
wildly.

"Keeley," he said softly, jolting her out of her
trance. "I had to see you."

She closed her eyes briefly and took a deep breath,
trying to slow down the acceleration of her heart. His
quietly spoken words shredded her heart to tiny
pieces.

"Please." He spoke again before she found her
voice. "Don't send me away."

Keeley tried to freeze him out, but it didn't work.
At his plea, her green eyes flew open and collided
with his warm blue ones. Pulled together by a force
neither one could deny, they found themselves moving closer.

Suddenly, Linc stopped, short of touching her. His
fingers curved into a tight fist as he said hoarsely, "I
didn't come here to—oh, damn!" he muttered disgustedly as he turned away and rubbed the back of
his neck. This action drew another oath from him as
it brought renewed pain to his sore body.

Keeley winced and stepped back. Stung by his apparent rejection of her and her momentary loss of control, she marshaled her defenses.

"I think you'd better go," she blurted out. Her
voice held a tremor in spite of her efforts to keep it
steady. As a further measure of self-protection against

the volatile attraction of this man, she drew the light-weight robe closer around her body.

Linc's eyes bored into hers. "No! I won't go," he said harshly, the lines around his mouth deepening. Then seeing the wild, frightened look that suddenly crossed her face, his eyes softened as he modified his statement a little. "What I meant to say is that I can't go, not yet, not until we've talked."

"There's nothing left to say," she stated flatly.

"Oh, I think there's a lot to say," he countered softly. And his eyes were saying it; they glittered like smoldering coals of fire as they sought the rich curves of her body that rested against the clinging fabric of her robe and gown. But he dared not move. The situation was much too delicate. I mustn't rush her, he warned himself.

"Please—"

Linc's eyes continued to hold hers. "Can't you find it in your heart to offer this weary athlete a cup of hot chocolate? If I promise to be on my very best behavior?" he asked in a husky tone, a beguiling smile lifting the corners of his wide mouth.

Keeley remained motionless, obviously searching for strength and the right words to make him leave. But much to her disgust, she continued to stand in one spot like a statue.

Would she be making a mistake if she fixed him only *one* cup of something hot to drink and then forced him out the door? Surely there could be no danger in that? At this moment, he looked as if it were taking all his reserved energy just to remain upright on his feet and talk to her. His description of himself, she thought, was grossly understated. The dark blue shirt he wore emphasized the swelling bluish-purple bruise under his left eye. Both his right hand and arm were wrapped in an Ace bandage.

"All right," she acquiesced ungraciously, "sit down. I'll only be a moment."

She whirled and stomped toward the kitchen only to come to a dead stop halfway as she heard a loud groan from behind her. She turned in time to see Linc, with a grimace of pain, lower himself onto the couch. Quickly she did an about-face and covered the short distance to the refrigerator where she yanked the door open, grabbed the carton of milk and set it on the counter. "Serves him right," she muttered under her breath as she banged around in the drawer looking for a spoon to mix the ingredients. Then she was immediately sorry for her unkind words and thoughts as she recalled the naked anguish she heard in his voice.

She wiped away the hot tears that had popped into her eyes with the back of her hand. She then zapped the hot chocolate mix into the microwave oven. While she waited, she leaned her head against the cabinet door and breathed deeply. *You're a fool, Keeley Sanders!* she berated herself. *A fool for allowing him to remain here. A fool for letting him continue to turn your world upside down!*

As soon as the microwave oven buzzed, signaling that its contents were ready, Keeley forced herself to move and complete the task at hand. Schooling her features to show none of her inner turmoil, she carried the tray into the living room and placed it on the coffee table in front of Linc.

This action brought no response. Looking up, she saw that he was sound asleep. For a moment, Keeley's eyes remained glued to his face, grimacing anew at the swollen jawbone and scratched nose. She noticed, too, how thick and long his eyelashes were and how they fanned in perfect harmony across his cheekbones. In spite of his roughed-up state, he appeared so vulnerable, so at peace. *No!* She shook her head. She mustn't let him get to her this way.

What now? Should she awaken him and send him on his way? she asked herself objectively. Or should she let him sleep a while longer? She ran a hand tiredly over her eyes and then looked down at the slender watch that circled her wrist. It was one-thirty. She groaned aloud. No wonder her body and mind refused to function properly.

Slowly Linc's eyes opened and for an instant he seemed not to know where he was. Then a dark scowl replaced his look of complete languor.

"Keeley, I'm sorry!" he muttered as he struggled to sit up straight. "Believe it or not, I didn't come here with the intention of passing out on your couch. I guess I was in worse shape than I thought," he added by way of an apology.

"That's all right. No harm done." Except to her heart and to her peace of mind, she thought with weary disillusionment.

A prolonged silence developed between them as Keeley lowered her head with the pretense of smoothing her robe. She felt sure Linc could hear her heart thundering against her chest as the silence deepened.

"May I still have a cup of that hot chocolate?" he asked, his voice low and sober. Not waiting for an answer, he reached for the container with the intention of helping himself. This action brought a quick response from Keeley.

"Wait—please. I'll pour it for you." Moving to sit beside him on the couch, but not too close, she leaned over and poured a cup of the rich chocolate liquid. Forbidding her hand to shake, she handed him the cup.

This brought another silence as Keeley watched with soaring impatience while he slowly sipped the drink. The china cup, she noticed, looked lost in his large hand as he purposefully savored every mouthful. From where she sat, she could smell the now recognizable brand of his cologne. Its tantalizing odor once again had the power to make her senses spin as did the protruding muscles of his thighs as they rested within touching distance of her hand. Panic flared inside her. Would this nightmare ever end?

When he had drained the last drop from his cup, he set it down on the coffee table and very gingerly stood up. Keeley rose simultaneously to stand beside him.

"Thanks," he murmured huskily, his eyes searching her face. "I guess you're right, lovely Keeley, about it being too late for us." A strange light appeared in the dark recesses of his eyes. "But I kept hoping—" His voice trailed off. "Oh, what the hell!" he muttered, following another agonizing moment of silence. "It doesn't matter now anyway."

Keeley caught her lower lip between her teeth to keep it from trembling. His eyes refused to release hers in spite of his soul-searching admission. He made no effort to hide the naked passion that now simmered from deep within them.

Her lips parted as she tried to speak. For a second time this evening, words refused to pass through her clogged throat. She remained motionless, her eyes held in bondage as her pulse began dancing to a wild and frantic beat.

"Shhh, don't say anything. No words are necessary," he whispered gently as though he understood her not being able to speak.

Suddenly, and of its own free will, a tear began a lone descent down her cheek. This was Linc's undoing. He groaned longingly as he reached out a finger and gently trapped it, refusing to let it wander at will.

His touch against her skin was like a lighted match carelessly thrown in a keg of dynamite. It created an explosion that neither was prepared for and neither was able to control.

She gasped as a quiver of liquid fire invaded her limbs. In that instant, she realized that nothing had changed. Linc Hunter still had the power to make her feel and respond like no other. Against her will, she found herself craving more of what he was so freely offering.

Taking her stillness as consent, Linc's fingers reached out and began to enchant her. They slowly and tenderly mesmerized the outline of her lips, parting them just enough to massage their inner sweetness. Keeley felt her legs threaten to buckle from the wave of burning desire that whipped through her body.

It was unclear who actually made the first move. All that seemed to be important was the urgent need to be in one another's arms.

Linc held her tightly against him as his hands moved up and down her back. Through the material of her robe, he could feel the exquisite contours of her body. He longed to peel the garment from her and stroke every naked inch of it until he had learned all its hidden secrets.

His kiss, when it came, was elusive. It was almost as if he were testing how far he could go and how much she was willing to give. He nipped at the corners of her mouth, using first his tongue and then his lips.

Keeley moaned and opened her mouth in hopes of trapping his teasing tongue. Realizing her eagerness, Linc kissed her full on the lips; tongues met and entwined as they feasted on the sweetness of the other's mouth.

When he freed her lips, Keeley touched him with trembling hands, making him groan and pull her down onto the couch. Then, she became the aggressor. She ran her hands through his hair, then gently fingered the inside of each ear. But she was careful not to touch with her hands the abrasions on his face. Instead she lightly caressed them with her lips.

"Keeley, Keeley—" he choked in a feverish voice as her gentle ravishment continued.

Her lips moved from this sensitive area down to the jutting boldness of his chin. As the roughness of his beard collided with the delicate softness of her lips, she rested there a moment and savored the taste of this delightful mixture. Her lips then trailed along the smooth skin of his neck—the only place left unscratched by human hands—and nibbled there. She then unbuttoned his shirt and pressed her palms into the thick mat of hair on his chest.

Linc's breath was coming in sharp spurts as she further appeased her curious fingers. His eyes were clouded with desire as he looked at her.

His large hands had ceased their roaming, enabling him to enjoy to the fullest the scorching quest of *her* hands as they freely prowled his body.

Then it was his turn. He kissed her hard with a hot, searing mouth and probing tongue. Linc's hands were as busy as his lips as he untied the sash of her robe and slipped it off. His fingers went to work on the tiny buttons that held her gown intact. When this task was done, he pushed it from her shoulders, freeing her breasts to his ardent gaze. Her breasts were beautiful. They were full and round and tilted in pouting readiness for his eager lips and tongue. The lamp, with its soft warm glow, caressed her milky white skin as Linc bent his head and took a nipple between his teeth. As if he had all the time in the world, he coaxed it into throbbing hardness before moving on to its companion.

Keeley's needs were growing, threatening to break the boundaries of self-restraint, as he left her breasts and moved back to her mouth. His lips fastened onto hers and deepened in infinite tenderness.

Not breaking the kiss, they sank together into the softness of the couch. In spite of his large sinewy frame, there was room for them both, so closely were they molded.

She could feel the boldness of him as they lay side by side with barely enough room between them even to breathe. In fact, Keeley felt certain they were breathing the same air as he drew the remaining oxygen from her lungs with his burning mouth.

Finally pulling back from her, he gently turned her sideways so that he had access to her breasts once again. As his mouth sipped there, a hand moved from her waist down to her thigh. He slowly began to lift her gown upward so as to have complete accessibility to all of her body.

The stirring hardness pressing against her other

thigh and the intimate wandering of his hand made Keeley suddenly aware of the precariousness of the situation.

Turning this fear into a reality were Linc's next words: "Keeley, I want you so much I'm not going to be able to stop," he muttered desperately.

This note of urgency sharply penetrated Keeley's drugged senses. Suddenly her body stiffened. Her eyes darted to Linc's face as she grabbed his hands and held them tightly.

"Keeley?" His eyes were glazed with pain.

"Linc, I—" She paused as her tongue circled her parched lips.

"Keeley, for God's sake! What's happened? I thought you wanted—" He couldn't go on. A desperate expression pinched his features as he fought for control.

She breathed achingly. "Linc, I—I think it's only fair that you know—" She swallowed convulsively. "I'm—"

"Keeley, what's wrong. Tell me!"

"I'm—I'm not on the pill."

His harsh ragged breath was the only sound in the deathly quiet room.

Hot burning tears scalded Keeley's eyes and cheeks as she turned her head aside. She waited for him to push her away. It was a proven fact that most men wouldn't tolerate this type of teasing behavior from a woman. Keeley was both mortified and embarrassed at her actions, both for her sake and his.

"Keeley, look at me," Linc demanded softly as he slowly turned her face back toward him. "Everything's going to be just fine." Her soul felt dissected under the sweet glow of his eyes.

"How—how can you say that after what I've done to you? To us?" The tears dripped in a steady stream down her cheeks.

"Shhh, don't cry. I can handle it, I promise." The tone of his voice was husky and warm.

"I'm—I'm not sure I can though," she hiccupped between sobs.

A deliciously sweet smile broke across his lips. "Then we'll just have to see what we can do about that, won't we?"

"But?"

"Shhh," he repeated huskily as he leaned down and began to lick the tears from her cheeks and lips. "Just lie still."

As Linc's lips played with hers, his hands began a tortuous descent down her body. They wandered from one breast to the other, downward to center stomach where a finger concentrated for several breathtaking seconds on the tiny delicate opening nestled there. Then ventured farther....

Keeley was finding it increasingly difficult to remain still under the talented manipulation of his fingers. Every nerve ending in her body quivered as Linc's hand reached the ultimate and final destination.

The contact was shattering. Her body tensed.

"Relax," he murmured, "relax and feel."

The soothing tone of his voice had the desired effect. The control to which she had so tenaciously clung disappeared like roses in the snow. Her body now lay broken into what seemed like a million pieces as she remained at the mercy of his expert hands.

She reached out and clung to the hard muscles of his shoulders and dug her fingernails into them as his hands began to move against her ever so smoothly. While they continued to bewitch her, he kissed her deeply. His tongue skimmed along the roof of her mouth and then tenderly sparred with hers.

As their lips finally parted, he whispered, "You feel so good—so beautiful there."

A tremor of excitement ripped through her lower body as she began to move to the steady rhythm of his unselfish hands.

His mouth, now locked on a nipple, sent a moan of pleasure through her lips. As the gentle assault continued with slow leisurely strokes, her moaning grew louder as her hips strained to meet the ever-increasing heat.

When she thought that both her mind and her body would surely explode, Linc brought her to the final and rewarding conclusion. Her loud cry of ecstasy as her awakening unfolded was partially smothered against his hard body as he gathered her close to his heart.

When it was over, Keeley lay utterly spent. What seemed like eons later, she managed to revive herself enough to collect her senses. Along with that revival brought the weight of what she had allowed to happen, crashing down upon her slim shoulders like a ton of bricks.

She began weeping on the inside as she pulled away from Linc and sat up. As best she could, she shifted her gown upward and covered her bare breasts. Linc, still behind her, didn't move a muscle.

With her heart swollen to the bursting point, Keeley rose and walked to the other side of the room. She had to put distance between her and Linc in order to think. But she just stood there, confused and frightened with nervous dampness oozing from her palms.

"Keeley, why aren't you taking the pill?" Linc's taut voice and probing question caught her completely off guard. For a moment, she thought her ears were deceiving her.

She whirled around and stared at him wild-eyed. "That's, that's none—" she began.

"If you're about to say it's none of my business, you can forget it!" he broke in harshly. The lines bracketing his mouth had deepened, and Keeley realized that he too was hanging on to his control by a thread. "What just happened between us *makes* it my business," he added, his voice now edged with unconcealed fury.

Instantly, the fight went out of Keeley. She felt her insides begin to crumble. Once more, she turned her back on him and fought for control. Why, she cried inwardly, did she continue to let herself succumb to his charms only to come out the loser? For surely as night followed day, she was exactly that—the loser. Her wanton conduct was like the taste of quinine in her mouth, bitter and revolting. And in the end, it would lead to nothing. So why did she continue to let him play havoc with her life in a way that she instinctively knew could bring her nothing but heartache?

Granted, his skillful hands had taken her down a path of forbidden delight from which she had never wanted to return, but that was still no excuse for her behavior. She would never forgive herself. As she stood, shaken to the depths of shame and despair, she had to admit that she had failed miserably when it came to forgetting him. Every time she allowed her heart to overrule her head, she tightened the web of deceit around her one notch tighter.

"Keeley?"

The coldness of his voice cut savagely into her tormented thoughts. She turned slowly around to face him. She saw immediately that the coldness in his voice matched that in his eyes.

"Keeley, I'm tired of playing games. It's too late for that now. So will you please answer my question?"

"I'm—I'm just not," she finally answered, her voice barely above a whisper.

But he had no trouble understanding her in the smothering silence of the room. "Why?" he asked simply.

"Because," she hedged.

"Because why?"

She took a deep breath. "Because, there's no need."

His eyes narrowed enigmatically. "Does that mean what I think it means?"

At Linc's words, Keeley's control deserted her. "Yes," she hissed at him as hot anger slithered through her. Why didn't he just leave her alone? Why must he humiliate her this way? "But rest assured that doesn't change things as far as we're concerned!" she added, her voice still tight with anger.

One eyebrow lifted. "Oh?"

Keeley bristled under his scrutiny. She was treading on thin ice and she knew it, but still she couldn't stop her next words.

"Don't 'oh' me, Linc Hunter! I don't owe you an explanation for anything I do!" Why am I shouting at him like this? she wondered hysterically. The blame rested on her shoulders, not his.

He was up and across the room before she could blink an eye. Pain or no pain, he had moved with the agility of a cat and now loomed over her, his hands clenched at his sides.

"How can you say that after what we've just shared?" he demanded, his nostrils tightening. "Didn't it mean anything to you?"

Keeley drew back, afraid of the darkening intensity of his face. Nevertheless, she refused to back down.

"Physically, yes, it meant something to me," she admitted. "Aren't actions supposed to speak louder than words?" Her voice was tinged with sarcasm and self-contempt. "But physical attraction isn't enough. I want more, much more than that, Linc. I refuse to have an affair with you or any man." She paused, giving her words time to sink into his hard head. "In spite of my actions and what you may think of me, I still plan to marry Jim."

"I don't believe you."

"It's true. Believe me, it's true. My life's all planned."

"I'll never accept that, Keeley. Not after the way you responded to my touch."

"Linc, don't do this—"

"Damn it, Keeley, don't shut me out! Give us a chance!"

"No! I can't." She spread her hands. "You just don't understand. I—"

"You're damn right, I don't understand!"

She tried again, this time stressing each word. "I've already told you, I'm going to marry Jim."

"I know what you said, but I don't believe—" he began heatedly.

Keeley raised her hands and placed one over each ear. "Don't say any more, please. Just go away," she whispered unsteadily.

A deep silence blanketed the room as Linc stood deep in thought. Keeley's back was turned to him, shutting him out. He had never felt so frustrated in his life. He longed to jam his hands into something hard, anything that would help to relieve the frustration that held him prisoner. But he knew that that kind of action wouldn't solve a thing. It would only bring renewed pain to his body and a string of expletives from his lips.

He wasn't used to women freezing him out. In the past, he was the one who did the breaking off. But this woman was different, and it infuriated him that he couldn't figure out what made her tick.

He recognized the fact that she was striving for an independence from her father's domination, as well as from the horrors of her past. Her biggest fear, or so it seemed to him, was not being able to stick to the carefully plotted course that she had mapped out for her life. She resented anything or anyone that might put a stumbling block in the path of her plans to marry her nice, steady fiancé who had a nice, steady job and could offer her a nice, steady, secure life. God! What a waste! he thought with disgust.

He looked at a partial view of her profile, and there was a haunting beauty about her that reached out to him and put a squeeze on his heart, causing him to become achingly aroused all over again. Her curls were in shining disarray around her face. From where he stood, he could see the tears sliding down her cheeks and the wobbling sweetness of her lips.

Watching her and remembering how she had responded to his touch, the deep purring sound of her voice and her deep cries of ecstasy as his hands had carried her to heights unknown made the blood pound through his body at an alarming rate of speed. Where would it all end? he wondered. It was madness! But a madness that had penetrated his body and refused to turn him loose.

He took a tentative step toward her and stopped. "I'm leaving now, Keeley," he said quietly. "But I'll be back."

With that promise ringing in her ears, Keeley heard the door click shut.

Five

It had been a week since Linc had walked out of her apartment. Keeley had lived each of those days in mortal fear. She hated to answer the doorbell or the phone and was even cautious when she stepped out of the house to go to work. But so far, there had been no word from Linc.

The night he left her, she broke down and cried far into the wee hours of the morning. Finally, just before daybreak, she fell into an exhausted sleep, only to awaken the next morning with her mind a seething cauldron of anger, bitterness and humiliation, directed solely at herself. How had it happened? How could she let him touch her in *that* way? Miserably she moaned over and over at how easily she let him conquer her body. No loving words passed through his lips. There was no need. She submitted without them. To deepen her mortification, each time her mind recalled the evening, her body ached with an intense longing.

Never a day went by that she didn't think about him and the way his mouth and hands tutored her body to crave his touch. She fought these thoughts relentlessly, but nothing she did seemed to help. Linc Hunter continued to fill her every waking moment. Even launching a full-scale attack on her work, demanding as much from her students as she gave of herself, didn't help.

As she straightened her desk and prepared to leave for the weekend, she realized how weary she was. Thoughts of the evening ahead loomed like an albatross around her neck. Jim was due in from Eugene at any moment, and they were to attend a dinner party at the home of Angela and Chad Kincaid. She sighed heavily as she rose from her desk and made her cursory glance around the classroom, making sure everything was in order for Monday morning.

Just as she reached for the blazer hanging on the back of her chair, she heard a light tap on her classroom door. She looked up and, to her amazement, saw Judith standing there.

Smiling, Keeley beckoned for her to come in and then crossed the room to meet her halfway. "My, but you're a sight for sore eyes on this Friday afternoon," she said as she leaned over and kissed Judith's creamy smooth cheek. "I'm pooped. How about you?"

Judith's smile was tense as she unloaded her shoulder bag on Keeley's desk. "I agree. I'm still in the early stages of convincing my fifth-graders that I'm the boss." She sighed. "On Friday they seem more hyper than any other time."

Instantly Keeley knew something was wrong. Judith's face showed none of its usual sparkle and vitality. And she couldn't remember ever hearing Judith complain about the students or her ability to cope with them. Something was definitely bothering her and Keeley knew that it wasn't job-related. Keeley felt a quickening of her own breath as Judith's unease communicated itself to her.

"Have a seat, Aunt Judith," she commanded, pulling out her desk chair and motioning for Judith to be seated.

Judith frowned. "Keeley, honey, I know you were getting ready to go home. I feel bad about bothering you after you've put in such a hard week."

Keeley perched on the edge of the desk and began swinging her foot in a relaxed manner, striving to put her aunt at ease. "Don't be silly, Auntie, I've got all the time in the world." She flashed her a sweet smile. "Don't you ever apologize for taking up even a minute of my time. If my memory is correct, this is the first time you've ever come to me wanting to talk." Her eyes became serious. "I'm honored. After all, I must owe you at least a million free counseling sessions," Keeley added with a grin playing around her mouth.

For a second, Judith gave an answering grin, and then it disappeared, leaving her eyes sad and troubled.

"What's wrong, Aunt Judith?" Keeley was extremely worried now.

Seeing the dark look that crossed her niece's face, Judith quickly lightened her expression. "It's really nothing serious—or at least not in the way you're thinking." She laughed, although it had a hollow ring to it. "I've always said there's no fool like an old fool."

Keeley felt her heart sink. "Aunt Judith, what on earth are you talking about? You're making absolutely no sense. Come on, out with it."

Judith's teeth worried her lower lip. "All right," she said reluctantly. "I've—I've been dating a nice man for some time now, and he's asked me to marry him."

Keeley's head snapped back as if she'd been

slapped in the face. She couldn't have been more stunned. She stared at Judith with her mouth open. Judith and another man? *That can't be! Aren't Judith and Dad...? Luther! Oh, God!* She reeled again as if from another blow.

"Keeley, please, don't look at me like that."

"Does my—my father know?" Keeley finally asked in a deflated whisper.

Judith shook her head. "No—no, he doesn't."

"I see," Keeley answered on a suppressed sigh. But she didn't see. She didn't see at all. And she didn't understand either. She was positive that she hadn't been mistaken about the way Judith had looked at her father. She couldn't have imagined it. Could she? Suddenly she felt ill.

"Keeley, you're making this all so difficult," Judith began, a pinched look to her features and tears glued to her lashes.

Keeley scooted off the desk and turned her back on Judith. She took deep gulping breaths to try and overcome the sick churning in her stomach. *What else can go wrong?* she cried despairingly.

"Keeley, please, don't turn your back on me," Judith pleaded. "Talk to me."

"Do you love him?" Keeley asked bluntly as she turned around. She studied her aunt quietly, trying desperately to understand her sudden change of heart.

Judith averted her eyes. "No."

Keeley felt a glimmer of hope flicker through her body. She relaxed. "Then I take it you aren't going to marry him?"

"No—what I mean is that yes, yes, I *am* going to marry him," Judith answered unequivocally.

Pain slapped her in the face. "Why? Why?" she stammered. "I—I was under the impression that..."

"That I cared for your father?" Judith finished the sentence for her with an unbecoming twist to her lips.

Keeley nodded. "Yes, that's what I meant," she whispered.

"Well, you're right, I do care. I care very much." She paused and ran a weary hand over her eyes. "But suddenly I'm tired of caring without anything in return."

"But, but—" Keeley sputtered incredulously. "You just can't give up now! Not after all this time!"

Judith's lower lip trembled. "Oh, yes, I can, my dear. I have no choice."

"Yes, you do—have a choice, I mean," Keeley replied in a frenzied tone. "You can say no to this man and mean it!"

Judith shifted uncomfortably. "Keeley, you must understand that your father sees me only as a good-hearted sister-in-law and nothing more. Over the past few months I've finally convinced myself of this." She sighed. "Now that your life's straightened out with plans to marry Jim, and Luther is well on the road to recovery, I'm—I'm no longer needed."

Keeley would have laughed at such a flagrant violation of the truth if it hadn't come from Judith's own lips. How could she be so blind? The day that she and Luther didn't need Judith would be the day they were both dead and buried.

"Aunt Judith, please, won't you reconsider? Think about it a little longer?" Keeley's heart was breaking. She couldn't help it. She had had her heart set on Judith's marrying her father. There had to be a way to get them together, she thought frantically, before it's too late. But how?

"Look," Judith said after a moment, "let's not talk about it any more this afternoon." She paused and looked down at her watch. "It's getting late, and I, too, have things to do." Her gaze softened as she looked at Keeley's distraught face. "Somehow, Keeley, darling, this is all going to work out for the best. You'll see. Just trust me," she added, a tiny smile pulling at her mouth. She then hugged Keeley fiercely before picking up her bag and walking out the door.

For a long moment, Keeley sat unmoving. It dawned on her that she hadn't even asked Judith the man's name or anything about him. Finally she forced her fatigued muscles to move. Suddenly, she was tempted to pick up the phone and call her father and tell him what he was about to lose because he was too blind to see beyond his own needs and desires. She was sure that Luther cared deeply for Judith and would never realize it until it was too late. But what could she do? Her hands were tied. Judith would never forgive Keeley if she divulged any of her aunt's plans to Luther. In matters of the heart, it had to evolve between the two parties concerned.

Nevertheless, as she left the building Keeley felt that everything just below the surface of her life was a welter of mistakes. She had made a mess of everything with her passion for Linc. Guilt over her disloyalty and deceit toward Jim and Luther remained a raging storm inside her. And now Judith was added to the list. Sadness weighed down her heart as she got behind the wheel of her Cutlass and drove home to prepare for the evening ahead.

* * *

"I hate this drizzle. I wish it would become a downpour and get it over with," Keeley remarked as she turned toward Jim. "Maybe by the time Angela and Chad's dinner party's over, it will have stopped."

But the rain was pelting down in solid sheets as Jim pulled up in front of her apartment several hours later. They waited a few minutes, thinking it would slack off. Finally, deciding it wasn't going to, they made a mad dash for the front door.

"Whew!" Jim exclaimed as they reached the warm interior of Keeley's apartment. "What a lousy night."

"I second that," Keeley returned, reaching for Jim's raincoat and hanging it up along with hers in the hall closet.

"Are you too tired for me to beg a cup of coffee?" Jim asked as he lowered himself onto the couch. "It seems as if we never have any time together lately."

To Keeley he suddenly sounded frustrated, tense. She felt an alarm signal go off in her brain. Was he aware of her withdrawal? Her evasiveness?

Trying to inject a little brightness in her voice, she said, "Make yourself comfortable and I'll put the coffee on to perk. Be right back."

The sound of the gurgling liquid followed Keeley as she made her way back to the living room. She plopped down beside Jim with a visible sigh and kicked off her shoes.

"Tired, baby?" Jim asked, reaching out and pulling her against him.

Keeley forced herself to relax, wanting too much to find enjoyment in his arms.

But suddenly Linc's haunting image appeared before her eyes with merciless clarity. She managed to stifle the groan that rose to the top of her throat, but couldn't stop herself from stiffening.

Then out of a sense of desperation, she buried her body closer to Jim's.

"What's the matter, baby?" he crooned. "Are you just tired, or is it something else?" He paused for a moment and moved his hand up and down her spine. "You seemed so uptight tonight...."

"I'm—I'm tired, that's all," she lied, at the same time making herself concentrate on Jim and his soothing voice and hands.

"What you need to do is stop working so hard, loosen up. I guarantee when we get married, you won't be working this hard," he told her, his lips grazing her warm cheek.

"I hope not." She sighed. If only she didn't feel so numb, so out of place, so confused.

Holding her close, Jim began to talk about the university, filling her in on the happenings there, forcing her to relax. Then he gently tilted her face up with his hand and laid his lips against hers. Gradually, as their lips molded together, the kiss deepened, and Keeley could feeling the rising heat of his body.

Keeley remained still in his arms with her eyes closed tightly, willing her emotions to respond. When nothing happened, she panicked. When Jim had kissed her in the past, she had always felt a sense of sweetness and contentment, but never this completely dead feeling inside her. Linc! Only Linc with his hands and mouth had the power to send flames of fire sizzling through her.

She recognized now that Jim was working to get her to return his ardent embrace. His hand was search-

ing for the fullness of her breasts when she abruptly
stilled his hand. She pulled away.

Jim opened his eyes and looked at her through narrowed eyelids. "What's wrong?"

Keeley floundered, opening her mouth and then
closing it. "I—I'm sorry."

"Sorry!" he repeated hoarsely. "Is that all you
have to say?"

Guilt quickly bloomed into frustrated anger. "What
do you want me to do?" Immediately she wished she
could recall those words. How callous! How stupid!
Of course, he wanted her to crave his touch. He
wasn't demanding more than any other redblooded
male would from the woman he planned to marry.

"I want you to love me," he snapped, emphasizing
how much she had hurt him.

"I want to, Jim. I want to so much," she cried, hot
tears filling her eyes.

Releasing his breath slowly, he stood up and strode
to the window to stare out at the night's inky blackness. After a moment of harsh silence, he spun around
to face her.

Deep sobs raked Keeley's body as she returned his
troubled gaze. "I'm so sorry. I—I promise I'll do
better next time."

He crossed the room and resumed his seat, cradling
her again in his arms. "Don't cry, baby. Listen, it's
all right. I understand. You're tired. I'm tired. There'll
be other times for us. The rest of our lives. Right?"

Keeley nodded wordlessly.

"Good. Now dry up those tears and walk me to
the door." He smiled sweetly into her face as he
reached out to brush the tangled curls from her wet
cheeks.

She grasped his hand and held it close to her face for a timeless moment, offering her silent thanks for his understanding. Then she stood up and walked with him toward the door. After retrieving his raincoat and pulling it on, he leaned over and kissed her reverently on the mouth.

"I'll call you later," he said as Keeley closed the door on his departing figure.

After securing the lock, Keeley trudged wearily to her bedroom, where she quickly shed her clothing. Suddenly, a chill shook her body as she methodically made her way to the bathroom and stepped into the shower.

As the hot water pelted her sensitive skin she tried to force the whole disastrous evening into the hidden recesses of her mind. It refused to budge from front center. In the beginning everything had been perfect: the food, the beautifully decorated table, the interesting conversation. Everything, except Keeley. A dull headache had plagued her throughout the whole evening, coupled with the nagging worry of Judith's unexpected bombshell. As a result, everything she had said and done was forced, even her smile. No wonder the remainder of the evening had turned sour.

As she scrubbed her body till it tingled she felt her frustrations increase. Did the solution to her problem with Linc lie in a hasty marriage to Jim? No! She shook her head helplessly. It wouldn't be fair to either of them, but most of all, not to Jim. What in heaven's name was she going to do if she couldn't stand for him to touch her? Damn! Linc Hunter had certainly done a number on her. Stop! Stop thinking! she reproached herself. What she needed was a good night's sleep. Tomorrow things will look brighter, she told herself as she reached over and switched off the bed-side lamp. She forced herself to count to a thousand twice before she fell into a deep and dreamless sleep.

With dawn's early light, Keeley opened her eyes. She knew something was different. She lifted her head with the intention of getting up, only to realize she couldn't. She was dizzy to the point of being sick to her stomach.

The remainder of Saturday Keeley stayed in bed, flat on her back, nursing a cold and sore throat that she guessed was the direct result of Friday night's outing. She made the perfunctory calls to her father and Jim advising them of her condition. Jim insisted on coming to her apartment and taking care of her, but she squelched the idea immediately, using the excuse that she didn't want him to catch her bug. Unwillingly, he agreed to go back to Eugene with a promise to call her soon.

By midday Sunday, she was feeling much better. She managed to keep down a bowl of hot chicken soup and several cups of hot tea. She was still weak but no longer nauseated or running a temperature. Her mind, however, was in a turmoil. The Timberjacks were playing the season opener against the Green Bay Packers. She wouldn't have gone to the game even if she'd been able, but it didn't keep her from wondering if Linc was being used as a punching bag again. She refused to turn on the television set.

In between lapses of worrying and napping, Keeley called her boss and informed him that she wouldn't be at work the following morning. She was positive that the extra day would render her one hundred percent recovered.

When the phone rang around nine o'clock, Keeley felt sure it was her father wanting to give her an account of the afternoon game.

Curling her feet up under her on the couch, she lifted the receiver. "Hello."

"Hello, lovely Keeley."

Her heart skidded to a stop at the same instant her hand froze around the receiver.

Ignoring her silence, Linc asked, "What were you doing?" His voice sounded tired, but pleasant.

"Re—recovering," she murmured.

"Recovering?" His voice sounded tense, worried. "From what?"

She sighed. "A light case of the flu, no doubt."

His harsh breath echoed through the line. "Are you sure you're all right? Have you seen a doctor? Do you need anything?"

"Hey, slow down." Keeley laughed. "I'm fine—just a little weak, that's all." New life pumped through her body at his show of concern.

"Are you sure?" He didn't sound convinced.

"Yes, I'm sure."

"Are you going to work tomorrow?"

"No—" she hedged. "At least I don't plan to unless I begin to feel stronger than I do now. Why?"

"I want to see you again." His soft-spoken confession ignited a need within her body that multiplied by leaps and bounds.

"Linc, I—"

"Keeley, I warned you I wasn't giving up, didn't I?"

"Yes, but—"

"Will you spend the day with me tomorrow?"

There was a long silence then.

"Keeley, please," he said, short of pleading. "This has been one hell of a week, and I'm starving for the sight of you."

Those words were enough to bring to the front of her mind in full vivid color the last time they were together. Memories of his hands and lips and the way he looked and smelled...

No! she moaned in silent misery. She couldn't let herself be lured into seeing him again by his velvet-soft words. She must cling to her vow to be strong.

"Keeley?" he persisted.

Her body jerked violently. "Linc, I can't."

"Do you want me to beg?" he asked harshly. "Will that make you happy?"

It was her turn to draw a harsh breath. "Don't, Linc. It won't work."

"Keeley, if you can honestly tell me—and I mean honestly—that you don't want to go with me tomorrow, you have my word I'll never bother you again." His words vibrated through the line like chips of ice hitting a tin bucket.

Instead of feeling relieved at his promised threat, she suddenly felt devastated. There was no doubt in her mind that he meant every word he had so carefully uttered. She quickly covered the receiver with her hand to keep Linc from hearing the half-strangled cry that escaped from her lips.

What was wrong with her that she couldn't end it all now? Here was her chance to rid herself of Linc Hunter once and for all! *Why am I hesitating like this?* she screamed to herself. This was what she wanted, wasn't it—for him to leave her alone—to disappear from her life forever?

"Goodbye, Keeley," he said quietly. "I'm sorry I bothered you."

Let him go! Hang up! This is your chance!

"No! Wait! Please—Linc, don't! Don't hang up."

There was another moment of shattering silence.

"Oh, Keeley," he breathed achingly, "it's times like this that I'd much rather throttle you than kiss you."

Hot tears scalded her eyes. "Linc—" Her throat caught the brunt of her weeping.

"Be ready at eight o'clock," he ordered before the phone went dead in her ear.

As Keeley sat holding the forbidding instrument, too startled to move, she realized with a calm certainty that, before her eyes, the plans for her future were being slowly dismantled like an old building, piece by piece, never to be rebuilt again.

She was ready and waiting when Linc rang her doorbell the following morning. She was dressed casually in a pair of blue pants and matching blue vee-necked sweater. Her hair surrounded her face in soft, shining curls.

Placing her emotions on ice, Keeley opened the door. But the instant their eyes collided, the ice in her veins melted, leaving her warm and trembling all over.

"Hello," she managed to eke out.

She could almost reach out and touch the tension that filtered the air as they stood still and let the memory of their last encounter come alive between them.

Keeley's eyes strayed to his hard mouth, the same mouth that had wreaked such havoc to her body, the same clean smell that had penetrated her skin, the same strong shoulders that had known her fingernails as she had gripped them in the throes of passion...

"God, Keeley!" Linc exclaimed. "Don't look at me like that or we'll never get out of this damned apartment." His eyes were liquid pools of passion as he stepped across the threshold.

Keeley's face burned with embarrassment as she quickly lowered her eyes. I'll have to do better than this, she thought, or I'll be in big trouble before the day ends.

They traveled in silence as Linc concentrated on the highway traffic. Keeley turned her gaze out the window. She saw that they were nearing the coast. Even if she hadn't been able to see the rugged beauty around her, she could identify it by the smell. There was nothing to compare with the tantalizing odor of the ocean. Its smell could get into one's blood, causing it to pound like the sea against the rocks. She had strolled the beaches along this coastline many times, and she never got tired of doing so. For her it never lost its charm or its beauty. She saw it as one of nature's best and unequaled wonders.

The silence stretched between them until Linc pulled into the small resort town of Cooper's Cove. This small dot on the map was one of Keeley's favorite places. She felt her excitement mounting as she itched to get out of the car and walk along the beach.

Suddenly she felt extremely happy. Happy that she was alive and happy that she was with Linc. At this moment she wouldn't trade places with another living soul. But on the other hand, neither was she a believer in fairy tales. The day of reckoning, she knew, would come with a stiff reprisal. Swiftly she pushed that thought to the back of her mind. She would cross that bridge when the time came and not a minute sooner.

"Well, we're here," Linc announced eagerly, yanking her back to reality.

"Great," she returned, excitement leaping from her eyes.

Linc grinned at her and then unexpectedly leaned across the seat and touched his lips to hers. At first his touch was as light and airy as a butterfly resting on a flower petal, but when Linc felt the slight tremor of her lips beneath his, he was lost. This gentle touch was not enough. He wanted more. Deepening the pressure, their lips clung together in a sweet burning passion that held them suspended in time.

"Linc, please—not here," she whispered achingly when she was finally able to dislodge his invading mouth.

"Why?" he murmured, still nipping tenderly at the corners of her mouth. "Nobody cares what we do," he added warmly as he sought to move closer to her.

"But I do," she wailed as she made an attempt to ward off his advance. Quickly she wedged her hands between them and then frantically searched for the strength to *keep* him at bay.

Linc lifted a hand that was planted firmly against the hard wall of his chest and started to nibble and suck the tip of each finger. Keeley felt her insides threaten to explode.

"Linc—don't," she began, only to stop and turn away from the scorching brightness in his eyes. Ignoring her plea, he continued the erotic play on her fingers.

"You can deny it until the world looks level, but

every time I touch you, your body begs for more, and you know it.''

Her eyes closed briefly as she fought against the overwhelming truth of his spoken words. She had no rebuttal. He had cut to the heart of the matter, leaving her absolutely no room to bargain.

As his warm chuckle vibrated in her ear, Keeley's eyes flew open. She saw the teasing twinkle in his eyes before he playfully tweaked the tip of her nose and then drew back from her.

''You can relax,'' he said with a grin. Then suddenly his expression became serious. ''Now's definitely not the time to prove to you that *you* belong to me.''

The moment Linc uttered those words he wished that he could have retracted them. He saw the frightened look that crossed Keeley's face. Damn! he cursed himself. What had made him say a thing like that anyway? *Get a grip on yourself, Linc Hunter, and remember your priorities! You're getting too involved with this woman—too close to her. Back off, before it's too late.* But somehow he thought those reprimands were already too late.

Keeley sat as though she were made of marble and stared at him, her lips slightly parted. Then she felt her heart and her emotions race and collide in wild disorder. How dare he make a rash statement like that! she fumed. Of course, he didn't mean it! It was merely a slip of the tongue. Belong to him? No way! Then why was it that each time she heard his voice or felt his touch, the mechanism of her structured life seemed to go out of order?

''Keeley, for God's sake, don't freeze me out again,'' he demanded hoarsely. ''Don't you think that this feeling between us doesn't scare the hell out of me too? Well, it does, but I know we've both got to come to terms with it sooner or later."

She lowered her head. "I—I know," she whispered, "but please—not—not now."

She felt his rugged breathing as he gripped the steering wheel tight. "All right, Keeley, I'll let you off the hook again this time, but oh, God, how I ache to hold you...." His voice was riddled with emotion.

Suddenly Keeley felt the need for fresh air. She groped frantically for the door handle. Linc didn't try to stop her.

When Keeley stepped from the car, the cool invigorating wind hit her cheeks and helped to restore her shattered emotions. She stood for a moment and breathed deeply as the sunlight danced on her skin. She forced herself to gaze at her surroundings—anything to take her mind off her surging needs. She noticed that Linc had parked the car in an out-of-the-way section of a beach called Shell Cove. It wasn't a popular tourist place because the sand was covered with shells and agates, which made sunbathing and swimming very uncomfortable.

As she looked around her, the place was totally deserted. Of course, it was a weekday, and the crisp nip of fall in the air was enough to discourage even the heartiest of beach lovers.

Keeley had been there several minutes before she felt Linc's presence behind her. Her heart fluttered.

When he spoke, his tone was warm but impersonal. "I think it's about time we soaked up some of this gorgeous sunshine, don't you?"

They strolled along the beach and gathered all the shells that Linc could cram into his pockets and windbreaker, before they headed in the direction of the restaurant. Linc's favorite eating place turned out to be a tiny cafe that was adjacent to the town square.

The checkered tablecloths and the smell of fresh-baked bread created an inviting warmth that wasn't present in most restaurants these days. As Keeley whiffed the delicious smell, she realized just how hungry the trek down the beach had made her.

"Well, how do you like it?" Linc asked as they were led to a table by the window by the jovial proprietor.

"It's absolutely delightful," she replied with a grin, "and the smell of that bread almost takes my breath away."

He laughed. "I second that. I'm about to starve myself."

They were handed a menu and then left to study it. There were so many delicious-looking dishes on the list that Keeley had trouble making up her mind. Finally she chose as Linc did, the broiled speckled trout with a baked potato and all the trimmings. Immediately they were served a miniloaf of hot bread with butter to munch on until their dinner arrived.

Linc cut her a slice from the loaf, covered it with a generous amount of butter and handed it to her. For a moment there was silence as they both appeased their empty stomachs.

At length, Keeley broke the silence as she swallowed her last bite of bread. "By the way, who won the game Sunday?" She shrugged. "I haven't had a chance to talk to Dad yet, so I don't know."

A strange look crossed Linc's face for a second and

then it was replaced by a mocking smile. "Do you really care?" he asked mildly.

Keeley was taken aback by the overtone of derision she heard in his voice. She stiffened. "Of course, I care," she countered defensively. "After all, I have a stake in who wins or loses."

His eyes narrowed. "You certainly couldn't prove it by me."

Keeley felt a blot of red sting her cheeks. Who did he think he was, trying to make her feel like a condemned woman just because she didn't get excited over a football game? She simply couldn't abide these men who were so wrapped up in sports that nothing else mattered. She had known all along that her and Linc's interests or goals in life weren't the same.

Instantly, she saw this whole day for what it really was, a lesson in futility. He would never change, and neither would she. The sooner she could overcome the intense physical attraction she felt for him, the better off they would both be.

"Keeley, please, look at me," Linc was saying. "I didn't mean to sound as if I was criticizing you." He paused and sighed deeply. "Believe me, I can understand why you feel as you do, but by the same token, you've got to understand that not every athlete is like Paul was."

"I'm aware of that," she stressed, her anger melting, "but it's all the other aspects of the sports world that I don't like. I despise the constant hounding by the autograph seekers, the newspapers, the constant limelight." She paused to push back a wisp of stray hair. "Although I will admit that there are times when I find it all terribly exciting, those times are few and far between," she finished dully.

"Keeley, I've already told you that I don't seek the limelight," he explained patiently. "But there are certain times when I have to do things that I don't particularly like."

"Linc, please, I don't want to discuss it anymore...." So much for bringing up his contract, she thought wryly.

She heard him mutter an expletive under his breath, just as their food was being placed in front of them.

The heavyset little man who had shown them to their table and had served the steaming hot food didn't seem to be in a hurry to leave. "You new around here?" he asked, his friendly eyes centered on Linc.

"Just visiting," Linc answered, his tone friendly enough, but it was obvious that his mind was elsewhere.

The man's smile widened as he peered closer at Linc. "I could've sworn I knew you from somewhere, but where I can't rightly remember." He paused to smooth the clean white apron that draped his protruding stomach.

Linc's smile remained plastered across his lips, but Keeley saw them tighten and a muscle begin to work in his jaw. He didn't say a word.

"Let me see," the man persisted, scratching his head with a puzzled look on his round face. "You wouldn't by any chance be that feller that quarterbacks for the Portland Timberjacks, now would you?"

Fighting hard to show none of the agitation that held his body taut, Linc, in one fluid movement, pushed his plate away and turned to the man and stood up.

"You're absolutely right," he said, holding out his right hand. "I'm Linc Hunter."

From that moment on, the tiny cafe was in shambles. Every patron that had crowded into the place for the noon meal clamored for Linc's autograph—kids and adults alike. As Linc followed the rowdy group up to the old-fashioned bar and countertop so as to have more room, Keeley noticed that Linc refrained from looking in her direction. He didn't want to see the "I told you so" expression she wore with both amusement and trepidation.

The timing of this autograph session is unbelievable, she thought, as she sat quietly and took it all in. She watched Linc as he charmed them all with his warm smile and teasing personality. It was hard for her to believe that he didn't enjoy meeting the public. His words of denial were meaningless now as he held the small audience captivated.

Once again fate came to her rescue with glaring clarity to show her just how futile her involvement with Linc really was. It wasn't so much this minor episode; somehow it seemed right that these people should have Linc's autograph. What it did point out was the large gap that existed between them. They were a part of two different worlds. Their relationship had no basis except sexual attraction, and that wasn't enough.

It was exactly one hour later when they escaped from the avid sports fans and made their way back toward the sand and the surf.

As they strolled along the beach, Keeley felt her eyelids become heavy. She certainly didn't want to spend the remainder of the afternoon behind drowsy lids. But she was hard pressed to hide the yawn that blanketed her features or make her relaxed limbs co-operate with her commands. The quantity of good food she had consumed was taking its toll.

"Hey, sleepyhead, you'd better wake up and watch where you're going," Linc teased warmly. "Or I'll be picking you up off the sand and then you'll be at my mercy."

A flush stole up her neck and into her face as she shot him a glaring glance. "You'd like that, wouldn't you? Watching me fall flat on my face, that is."

His chuckle deepened. "No, actually I wouldn't like to see you fall on your face, but I sure would like having you at my mercy." His eyes danced mischievously as he peered down into her upturned face.

Keeley knew he was teasing her, but nevertheless, she felt her heart race madly at the meaning behind his words. Not wanting things to get out of hand again, she completely ignored his innuendo and increased her pace. He just isn't content to keep his mouth closed, she fumed inwardly.

She heard his deep, throaty laughter as it echoed off the billowy force of the wind. It was only a moment before he caught up with her. Still determined to head off any personal or intimate conversation with him, Keeley rushed to say the first thing that came to mind.

"What do you plan to do when you quit playing football?" she blurted out, then wanted to bite her tongue off for asking such a personal question. Still, she waited impatiently for his answer.

He stared at her oddly for a moment before turning his gaze toward the water. "I don't like to think about that day ever coming," he stated soberly.

Keeley refused to stop and analyze why her heart

lurched from hearing his words. But something inside goaded her on. "Surely you must know you can't play football forever!"

A dark, inscrutable mask slipped over his face. "Nothing is forever, lovely Keeley," he parried evasively.

She shook her head helplessly as her frustration mounted. She felt like she was playing a game of tug-of-war as she tried to get him to talk about himself. Is he just being coy? she wondered. Or is he trying in a tactful way to tell me that his future plans are none of my business? Which, of course, they aren't, she reminded herself with brutal candor. But either way, she felt driven to get an answer out of him.

"I know," she answered flatly, "but I also know that you can't keep letting your body get battered and bruised time and time again without paying the consequences." She paused to dust a spot of sand from her pants. "It's impossible to hide the grimaces every time you make an unexpected move. It's obvious that your limbs are registering a protest."

His eyes were steel-coated as they whipped around to stare at her. "Is this interest in my career and my life personal, or has Luther been up to his old trick again of trying to let you negotiate my contract?" His softly spoken words had the same effect as a smack across the head.

Keeley lifted shocked green eyes to stare at him. How dare he insinuate either of those things? His egotism was unmatchable! Then just as quickly as her anger surfaced, it subsided. It was she, not Linc, who was at fault. She had indeed overstepped her bounds by grilling him with questions about his career and remarks about his body. No wonder he was defensive. He had every right to be.

Her eyes dipped to the ground to hide her embarrassment. "I'm—I'm sorry," she apologized, her voice faltering. "I had no right to…"

"Keeley, look at me," Linc demanded, stopping abruptly and tilting her face up with his hard, warm fingers.

It took every ounce of her willpower to face him. And still her pride lay in tattered shreds as her eyes anxiously centered on the rugged planes of his face.

Linc hadn't removed his fingers. Using his thumb, he began to seesaw back and forth across her chin. Everywhere he touched, Keeley felt as if hot needles were prickling her skin.

"You have every right to ask me anything you want," he said in a torture-ridden voice. "Since the first moment I laid eyes on you, I haven't been the same. I want you now so badly it's ripping my guts to pieces."

"Linc—" She closed her eyes against the pain in his eyes that was mirrored in her own. I asked for this, she thought unhappily. She had no one to blame except herself.

His lips compressed into a thin line. "I know what you're going to say. You're committed to another man and I'm committed to football." He sighed heavily. "But damn it, Keeley, there's got to be a way for us to work all this out."

She shook her head. "There's—there's nothing to work out," she stammered. "You have your life and I have mine—with Jim," she added in a throaty whisper.

Before she realized his intention, his arm shot out

and in a jerking motion pulled her up against his hard length. Her lips parted in shocked dismay at the sudden turn of events.

"Does your safe and secure Jim have the power to make your heart hammer and your pulses race like they're doing right now?" he ground out harshly. "And do your breasts swell with longing and your nipples harden with desire when he touches you? Answer me!"

Keeley couldn't have answered him even if she'd wanted to. Her head was spinning from the wanton emotion that threatened to swamp her. She could feel the throbbing fever of his passion as he held her tightly against him.

When his lips found hers, they were as hot and searing as his words. She felt on fire from head to foot.

The kiss ended almost as quickly as it began. When he pushed her away from him, she clung to his arm in self-defense before she felt the strength return to her limbs.

The wind whipped about them as they held their positions, both too shaken to move.

"Come to Bend with me?" he murmured in a strangled tone.

She felt like a storm had ripped through her body and left it shattered to pieces. She heard Linc's voice, but the words didn't sink into her saturated senses.

"What—what did you say?" The quiver in her voice reduced it to a mere whisper.

"I want you to go with me to Bend in about two weeks," he repeated, measuring his words as his eyes continued to hold hers.

She tried to dispel the strange disoriented feeling

that clung to her. She shook her head violently.
"Bend? What's in Bend?"

"My ranch."

"Ranch?"

An exasperated smile crossed his lips. "Yes, ranch.
A horse ranch to be exact."

"Oh."

Linc burst into laughter, helping to shatter the
charged-up atmosphere between them. "Is that all
you have to say?"

Suddenly, Linc's words penetrated her numbed
brain, causing her to reel from its impact. Linc owned
a ranch? A horse ranch? She couldn't believe it! But
it has to be true, she thought wildly, or he wouldn't
have issued this bold invitation for me to visit it.

"Let's walk," Linc said briskly, "before the wind
picks us up and carries us off." A faint smile twisted
his lips as he ducked his head.

Keeley felt her legs move of their own accord while
her thoughts remained in a chaotic mess. For some
reason, Linc's admission disturbed her. Why? she
wondered. Was it because he was no longer just a
football player with no real ambition in life except to
play football? Now she was seeing him in a totally
different light. Why was that so unsettling?

Before she had a chance to search her mind for
answers to those provoking questions, Linc's next
words crashed in on her thoughts.

"If you'd take that Friday off from work, we could
leave that morning and have the whole weekend to
stay at the ranch."

"No, Linc, that's impossible," she told him without hesitation.

He stopped once again and spun around, exasperation snapping in his blue eyes. "You've got to be the most stubborn woman I've ever known, Keeley Sanders!" He paused, obviously trying to get hold of his emotions.

The wind was stronger and colder now as it whipped off the water. Their rambling along the beach wasn't nearly as pleasant as it had been earlier in the afternoon.

"I think we should make our way back toward the car," he suddenly advised, his tone bitingly blunt. "We can finish our conversation there," he added.

Keeley nodded without replying as they turned and began their trek down the long stretch of beach, her thoughts in a whirl. Bend! She couldn't go to Bend. Even the thought was ludicrous. Linc was sure to demand an answer. Of course, it would be no, unequivocally no. She also knew that Linc wouldn't give in without a battle. But this time she would be strong and make the no stick.

Six

Exactly one week later, Keeley still hadn't reached
a firm decision whether or not she was going with
Linc. The constant worry over their stormy relationship haunted her day and night. As if that weren't
enough, she was under pressure from Jim to set a date
for their wedding. Since their last encounter, he had
become more aggressive and pushy. Also the knowledge that Judith was still seeing the other man bothered her tremendously. She had managed to avoid
both her father and Judith that week. She was having
difficulty handling her own problems much less
theirs. But unfortunately, both her excuses and her
time had finally run out.

She was due to meet Luther at his office in the
dome stadium in five minutes. The doctor had reluctantly allowed him to go to work for two hours a
week. As Keeley parked her car and walked toward
the outside entrance to the offices, she tried to dispel
some of the gloom that hung over her.

Forcing a smile for Luther's secretary, she crossed
the threshold into his office. He sat at his desk peering
over the ledger. He looked up with a scowl on his
face.

"I've dangled about as much money as I intend to
in front of Hunter's face," he said without preamble.

"I finally got in touch with his agent and made what I hope is my final offer." He slammed the ledger closed. "I can't understand what he's holding out for. I know for a fact he's not talking to any other teams."

Keeley ground her teeth together as she plopped down into the chair in front of Luther's desk. "Dad, I *know* that Dr. Willis didn't intend for you to do any bargaining with the players." She expelled an impatient sigh. "That wasn't at all what he had in mind when he told you that you could come to the office a few hours a week. You're just trying yourself!"

He thrust her words aside with a wave of his hand. "Well, you certainly haven't done your part in trying to get Linc's name on another contract, have you?" Before she could answer he hammered on relentlessly, "You haven't made any overtures toward seeing him *again* or talking to him, have you?" His eyes challenged her to find fault with his accusations. "No. I can answer for you. You've done nothing. Absolutely nothing! So *I had* to take the initiative," he finished forcefully.

Keeley felt her face suffuse with color as she lowered her gaze to her lap. How she hated this type of deceit! But how could she tell him that not only had she seen Linc but that his hands and lips had traversed her body and brought her to unimagined heights? And that no matter how hard she tried, she couldn't stay away from him? And that Linc felt he could afford to hold out for a better contract because of his relationship with the owner's daughter? *No!* She could never admit these things to him. His weak heart would never sustain the blow.

Composing her features to hide her raging thoughts, she raised her eyes to meet his. "Please,

Dad," she pleaded, "just do what the doctor ordered. I don't want you to have to go back to the hospital because you're too stubborn to listen to reason."

Surprisingly, her plea seemed to have scratched the surface of his determined attitude. He suddenly relaxed and threw her a rather sheepish smile.

"Quit your worrying, girl. I'm not about to land myself back in the hospital. So wipe that concerned look off your face. Anyway," he added with a grin, "I'm not about to let anything interfere with my pleasure of having the hottest team in the N.F.L."

She smiled. "I'm glad to hear that. Just make sure you stick to it."

"I'll try," he said with a grin. Then his grin faded abruptly, leaving another troubled look on his face.

"Dad?"

He thumped his pencil on the desk for a second before saying, "Have you talked to Judith lately?"

Keeley felt her heart turn over. "Yes—yes, I have," she admitted reluctantly. "Why?" She had to ask, but she dreaded hearing the answer.

His eyebrows puckered. "Well, I can't put my finger on it, but something's wrong." He shrugged. "She doesn't come by the house nearly as often as she used to, and when she does, she acts strange." His eyes clouded. "I know it's not just my imagination either. She's different, and it worries me," he added on a dejected note.

Keeley breathed an inward sigh of relief. At least he isn't asking me for a confirmation, she thought. She couldn't bear to tell him about Judith's plans. That must come from Judith. But she was glad to see that her father was aware that her aunt was no longer at his beck and call. Her mind began clicking. Maybe it wasn't too late for them after all, especially if she prodded her father a little.

"Dad, has it ever occurred to you that Aunt Judith might be trying to make a life for herself, aside from you and me?" Her breath hung suspended in midair as she waited for the answer.

His eyes became narrowed slits. "You trying to tell me something, girl? If you are, spit it out."

Keeley licked her suddenly dry lips. "No!" she said quickly, before she lost her nerve. "It's just that Judith deserves a home and family of her own. After all, she's given us the best years of her life." She paused to let her words soak in. She noticed that Luther's face looked as dark and threatening as a thundercloud.

In what she hoped was a neutral and unconcerned voice she went on, "Anyway, maybe she found something or—someone to take our place."

"Like hell she has!" he bellowed as he sprang out of the chair and turned his back to her. After a moment of silence, he turned around to face her. "I can see right now it's time Judith and I had a talk. In fact, it's long overdue."

Keeley hid the smile that poked her lips. She had planted the seed, and that was all she could do. Now it must take root and grow. She just hoped her good deed hadn't come too late.

After discussing several business transactions with her, Luther left to go down to the training rooms and visit with the players who were working out. Linc probably wasn't one of them, she thought with a strange pang.

She was buried deep in writing down the results of several phone calls she had made for Luther when she heard the door open. Thinking it was her father, she kept on writing.

"Back so soon? Too bad there wasn't anyone working out," she babbled. When she received no answer, she jerked her head up. Her heart slammed up into her throat.

Linc!

"Hello, lovely Keeley," Linc said quietly as he raked his eyes over her with a slow, thorough boldness that made her pulse jump.

"Hello," Keeley answered breathlessly.

Linc smiled, his smooth gait moving him quickly across the room. He stood undaunted, directly in front of her, his expression unchanged.

Keeley dared not move. The desk between them served as a stalwart shield to ward off any further advances from him. It also served to hide her trembling hands and legs.

She eyed him warily as he maintained his poised stance. His hands were crammed in the pockets of his athletic shorts, and his shirt was casually unbuttoned, showing the light curling hair on his broad chest. He smelled of cologne and soap, and her gaze was helplessly glued to his clean-shaven face.

"Are you going with me Friday morning?" he asked, his voice low and disturbing.

Keeley felt a response to his gentleness stir in the base of her stomach. She realized that the time of vacillating between "Yes, I'm going" and "No, I'm not going" had suddenly come to an end. Linc expected an answer—now. From all appearances, he looked calm and rational, but she knew that underneath that composed facade, he was smoldering like a volcano ready to erupt at a moment's notice.

She made the pretense of closing the notepad and straightening Luther's desk. She had to do something to stall him. She needed more time.

But she wasn't fooling Linc; he knew exactly what she was up to. With liquid-smooth agility, he reached over and covered one of her busy hands with his. Her other hand immediately halted, ceasing its petty wanderings.

Without thinking, Keeley's glance flew up to his face, so very close to her own now.

"You're stalling, and we both know it," he pointed out sharply. His eyes, stained with dark and menacing impatience, bore down into her.

"Linc—" She broke off to wet her dry lips.

"Linc, what?" he persisted meaningfully without altering his close position.

Keeley could see a muscle working overtime in his jaw, which was held in a tight clench. She focused her eyes on that one spot and groped for the courage to tell him to go away, but the words died in her throat. Then Judith's words of warning suddenly flashed across her brain like a neon sign: "Remember physical attraction can be a strong stimulant." That was the crux of the matter, a feverish physical attraction. She was caught in its power like grass under a withering, hot sun. She had no place to hide from its all-consuming force.

"Keeley—" he warned, his top lip curled back.

"All right! I'll go, but damn you, Linc Hunter! Damn you!" Her voice literally cracked with all the pent-up longings and frustrations that had festered for so long inside of her.

For a minute the room was like an ominous cloud

of silence, threatening to smother them both with its violence.

Then suddenly, to add insult to injury, Linc threw his head back and laughed out loud.

"You'll be glad to know your wish has already come true, lovely Keeley, that I've been damned for a long time now and living in hell to boot!"

Leaning over, he swiftly kissed her parted lips and added calmly, "I'll pick you up Friday morning at ten."

Fifteen minutes later she was still fuming at Linc's ability to mold her like a piece of soft clay any way he saw fit. And what was even worse, she let him get away with it! Somehow she managed to pull herself together enough to leave. Making her way out the door, she almost bumped headfirst into her father.

"Keeley, for heaven's sake, watch where you're going!"

"I'm—I'm sorry, Dad," she apologized unsteadily, "but I just remembered something important that I must take care of." She patted his cheek absently. "I'll call you later," she flung over her shoulder as she pushed her legs at breakneck speed to leave the office.

That *something of importance* was a need to talk to Aunt Judith.

Because of this urgency, she failed to note the taut white line that surrounded Luther's mouth or the gray pallor of his skin. He watched with a bitter twist to his lips and drooping shoulders as Keeley made a speedy exit.

The drone of the twin-engine Cessna as it flew over the Cascade Mountains toward Bend, Oregon, made conversation impossible. It's just as well, Keeley thought as she pressed her nose against the window and tried her best to see the terrain through the clouds and haze. She didn't feel like talking anyway. She had become suddenly tongue-tied around Linc.

The moment he arrived at her apartment, a feeling of intense apprehension tightened her stomach. But then she had quickly reassured herself that nothing could happen between them that she didn't want to happen. She was in command. She could control the situation. It was just a matter of self-will and determination. Reminding herself of this made it possible for her to live with herself after giving in to Linc *again*. Even her lengthy talk with Judith following her flight from Luther's office had failed to give her the answer that she needed concerning this trip. Her thoughts had remained a jumbled-up mess of contradictions for days afterward. But in the end, the decision sat squarely on her shoulders. She prayed in earnest that she had made the right one.

Thrusting these unsettling thoughts aside, she turned and ventured a look in Linc's direction. He was totally occupied with piloting the plane and oblivious to her presence. He certainly seems to be in complete control of the Cessna, she thought. She smiled to herself as she remembered how her mouth had flown open when she learned that he was planning to fly them to his ranch. It proved to be another contradictory side of this talented and versatile athlete who occupied all of her thoughts.

Sensing her unrest, Linc reached across the middle panel and gave her hand a gentle squeeze. "Relax, honey, I promise you we won't fall out of the sky."

He threw her a lopsided grin before turning his attention back to the controls.

She gave him a brief smile in return and then continued her perusal of him out of the corner of her eye. He was comfortably dressed in a pair of jeans and knit shirt. She noted with relief that he had managed to come through Thursday night's game virtually unscratched.

The Timberjacks had kept their record unmarred by beating the New England Patriots. The final score had been twenty-eight to zip. Linc, as usual, had been his dazzling self. Before the game ever started, Keeley had kept telling herself that she wasn't going to turn on the television set, but when eight o'clock rolled around, she had punched the button as if she were automatically programmed. She had rationalized by promising herself she would only watch a few minutes of the game. But when she had heard Howard Cosell in the pregame show talking about the Timberjacks' stunning quarterback and the fantastic year he was having, she had been hooked. She hadn't missed a minute of the play-by-play action.

"My, but you're awfully quiet," Linc said, breaking into her deep introspection. "Not still having second thoughts about coming, are you?" He spoke louder than usual to make himself heard above the roar of the engine.

Her lips curled expressively. "No, as a matter of fact, I'm glad." She leaned her head closer toward him to keep from having to strain to talk to him. "I know you're finding that hard to accept, but it's true." Admitting this to herself was a major step, but confessing it to Linc...

Her smile turned into a soft laugh, showing off her

even white teeth and dimples to perfection. Linc found himself swallowing hard as his eyes drank in her loveliness. She looked utterly delightful in a pair of gold-colored slacks with a matching shirt and blazer. Her soft curls that fell about her shoulders were soft and luxurious. When she had leaned close to him, he smelled the vibrant scent of her body, making him want her with a craving that frightened him. Damn! he cursed to himself. He was in for a very long and uncomfortable weekend if she held him to his promise not to demand from her what she wasn't willing to give. Why had he made such a rash statement? He was wondering now if he would be able to honor it.

Shortly thereafter, Linc began preparing for the descent. In the small plane, the definite drop in altitude was sorely felt. Quickly, Keeley forced her mouth apart and swallowed several times to try to unstop her ears.

Linc landed the plane at the small Bend-Redmond Airport and taxied to a stop. Although Keeley had visited this very popular resort town located at the edge of the Deschutes Mountains, it had been years ago. She found herself looking forward to Linc's promised threat of the hike through the mountains, which were beautifully inviting.

Keeley suddenly felt happy and carefree herself and a little giddy that she had done something forbidden and totally out of character for her. So totally out of character, in fact, that she hadn't told anyone where she was going except Judith. Not Jim. Not her father. Thinking of Luther now, however, brought a twinge of uneasiness to mind. She had spoken to him briefly on the phone concerning a business matter and he had sounded strained, upset. She had asked him if he was feeling all right, only to have him snap back at her that he was just fine. At the time, she had attributed his abruptness to his usual depression and disgust over his illness, in addition to his nagging worry about Judith.

But now she wasn't so sure. The more she thought about it, the more convinced she was that something else was wrong. But what?

Luckily Linc's smiling face relieved her mind of this dark and intruding thought.

"I'm ready when you are," he said, grinning.

Keeley flashed him a bright smile. "What are we waiting for, then?" she quipped. "Let's be on our way."

As they drove from the airport through the town Keeley looked closely at her surroundings. The early October day was chilly but sunny. As they traveled through the beautiful wooded area on the sweeping curve of the Deschutes River, Keeley inhaled the fresh scent of lush pine trees that graced the slopes of the mountainsides. She felt again a low rumble of excitement surge through her insides at the thought of tromping through those wild, lush forests with Linc as her only companion.

Turning toward him, she cocked her head to one side and said, "It just occurred to me that I don't even know where your ranch is located." She blinked her eyes. "All I know is that it's somewhere around Bend," she added hesitantly.

He grinned boyishly. "I think you'll be pleasantly surprised. It's beautiful, but then I'm prejudiced." His eyes swept over her face. "Actually, the ranch is in

Tumalo—about seven miles northwest of Bend. I raise and train Arabian horses.''

"It sounds like paradise." She sighed softly.

Thirty minutes later, Linc stopped the car outside a long and heavy gate with the words Hunter's Horse Ranch branded on it. He energetically bounded out of the car and had the immense gate out of the way within seconds.

Lowering his muscular body behind the wheel once again, he threw a grin in her direction. "Well, you are about to see where I spend all my time when I'm not pounding the gridiron." Suddenly his voice sobered. "This place runs deep in my blood. I love it here." Keeley's eyes followed his, taking in the lush green beauty of the ponderosa pines that stood tall and unbending in the foreground; then her eyes swept over the Arabian horses as they stood majestically in the distance, swishing their tails in proud nobility.

It was on the tip of Keeley's tongue to ask him why, if he loved it here so much, he didn't give up football and stay. But she held her tongue, not wanting to shatter the contentment that existed between them. Instead, she turned to him and smiled. "I can see why you're so proud of this place. It's absolutely breathtaking."

"I'm glad you approve," he said, sounding relieved. "I love my horses almost as much as I do football." He paused as a sheepish grin crossed his face. "Well, almost as much," he added dryly.

She laughed without humor. "You didn't have to tell me that, Linc Hunter. You've made it quite plain where your heart lies." She hoped that he wouldn't catch the disjointed sound of her voice.

His eyes were gentle as they rested on her. "Don't

be too sure of that, lovely Keeley,'' he advised
mildly.

Keeley felt as though her breath was trapped in her
lungs as she turned her head away from the warmth
of his gaze. Surely, she told herself, he didn't mean
what his words intimated. But even if he did, it was
only physical yearnings and nothing more. Their relationship was on a road to nowhere. She had to keep
that thought uppermost in her mind.

"Do you ride?" he asked eagerly.

She hesitated. "A little, although it's been quite a
while since I've done so," she added hurriedly.

"Well, it won't take long for you to get back into
the swing of things," he predicted as he guided the
car over the rutty road. "I have the perfect mount for
you." His eyes twinkled. "One that I promise won't
pound your underside too much."

"Thanks for nothing!" she retaliated sarcastically.

He threw back his head and laughed as he removed
a hand from the steering wheel and tweaked the end
of her nose playfully.

She found herself returning his grin in spite of her
effort not to do so, and for a timeless moment she let
herself wallow in the glowing warmth of the camaraderie that hung so tenaciously between them.

Suddenly, Linc pointed to her right. "There's my
one and only corral, but as you can see it's rather
large. I hope in the not too distant future to have two
more." He shrugged. "I've only owned this place for
three years. I'm just now beginning to get it in
shape."

"I'm impressed," she acknowledged as her eyes
followed his pointing finger. "Who takes care of all
this for you during the football season?"

"I have a couple who shoulder all the responsibility of the ranch, plus several general ranch hands. You'll meet Hazel and Duffy shortly."

As he uttered those words, the car halted abruptly in front of what looked to Keeley like a small, but extremely attractive, house painted a dull gray with bright yellow shutters. A wide porch spanned the front of it. She fell in love with the place immediately.

"Do you like it?" Linc inquired as he took in the rapt expression on her face.

"Oh, yes," she breathed. "I think it's utterly charming."

"Good, but unfortunately I can't take much of the credit. Hazel is responsible for just about everything, including the color of the paint."

"If that's so, I can't wait to meet her."

As Linc came around the car and opened the door for her, Keeley noticed at once the pungent smell of horses combined with the fresh pine scent that drifted down from the nearby hills and mountains. She wrinkled her nose as Linc joined her. It seemed the most natural thing in the world for him to drape his arm around her shoulders as they strolled unhurriedly toward the house.

Keeley felt her breath stick in her throat as her breast teased the side of his ribs. It was as if their every movement was synchronized in perfect harmony. Did he notice? she wondered as his hands slowly but absently caressed her shoulder blades.

None too soon for Keeley's peace of mind they reached the front steps only to have the door flung back with a bang. In fact, Keeley was amazed that the hinges remained intact.

"It's about time you showed up, you young scal-awag! I had given you up for lost!"

Keeley's eyes brimmed with shock as a grossly overweight woman, who she assumed was Hazel, grabbed Linc around the waist and gave him a bear hug.

"You're a sight for sore eyes," Linc gushed affectionately, returning the woman's embrace twofold. "As usual you're wasting away to nothing," he added playfully as he grabbed a roll of fat bordering her waistline.

"Huh! One of these days you're going to regret those words, you young devil!" She then batted his hand away and disentangled herself from his arms. "Beats me why I put up with the likes of you."

Turning, she noticed Keeley. She squinted her eyes until they were merely narrow slits bracketed by ounces of fat and took in every detail of Keeley's appearance. A grin covered her entire face as she held out a hand.

"I'm Hazel Grimes," she said by way of an introduction. "And you must be Keeley."

Keeley smiled as they shook hands. "I'm pleased to meet you, Hazel."

"Same here," Hazel announced abruptly, but Keeley took no offense. She knew she had passed the test and won Hazel's immediate approval. Why that should please her so, she dared not question.

During the exchange, Linc stood to the side taking it all in with an amused grin on his face. He breathed an inward sigh of relief that Hazel approved of Keeley.

Following Hazel inside the house, Keeley paused briefly and looked around. With one engrossing sweep, everything registered in her mind's eye: the living area with its warm atmosphere, the cheerful but clinically clean kitchen and the large dining area that adjoined it.

"God, it's good to be home," Linc expressed, torrid longing deepening his voice.

"I envy you this to come home to," Keeley countered bleakly as her eyes continued to canvass the room.

Linc felt an uncontrollable quiver jerk through his body at the haunting sadness he saw reflected in her eyes. He longed to hold her close and promise her that nothing or no one would ever hurt her again, but he couldn't do it. He was afraid that that type of action would send her defenses shooting up again. So he continued to stand there, feeling as though his legs were encased in a steel trap, and let the ache of wanting her drive him deeper into pain and despair.

He shifted his weight, hoping to bring solace to his aroused body, when suddenly the hinges on the front door were tested once again.

Keeley spun on her heel and took in the man who, like a tornado, came through the door. His thin weathered face was one big smile.

"Linc, my boy, it's good to see you," the man said as he pumped Linc's hand up and down.

"Same here, Duffy," Linc echoed, a warm grin covering his features. "You and Hazel are a sight for sore eyes."

"Sure makes me and the missus proud the way you've been throwing that football." His blue eyes gleamed underneath bushy brows. "Goes to show, you ain't lost your touch. Keep givin' 'em hell!"

Linc laughed heartily before giving the old man's

shoulders a final squeeze. "Duffy, I'd like for you to meet a special friend of mine." Turning, he reached out and grabbed Keeley's hand and pulled her next to him, circling her waist with his arm.

Even this passionless encounter had the power to ricochet a need throughout her body. She fought to master her loss of control as she smilingly shook hands with Duffy. She hated herself for going soft every time he touched her. At this rate, she wouldn't be able to make it through this weekend without doing something foolish.

For the remainder of the day and the evening, Keeley made it a point to stay away from Linc, and to her satisfaction, she found it comparatively easy to do so without being obvious. It seemed that either Hazel or Duffy or both were with them constantly. Hazel insisted they eat lunch before doing anything else. Against her better judgment, Keeley complied with her insistence but drew the line at consuming a bowl full of strawberry shortcake topped with whipped cream.

The afternoon was spent walking and looking at part of the ranch and watching Linc work on breaking a colt. The entire time Linc sat astride the untamed horse, Keeley's heart remained somewhere in the vicinity of her throat. She was positive that the horse would get the best of him. It seemed to her that Linc was hellbent on destroying himself either atop a wild animal or through bone-jarring contact on the football field.

But that was the only incident that marred the day, and it didn't last long. Linc noticed the pallor of her skin and willingly gave up the endeavor. By the time the hands of the grandfather clock rolled around to ten o'clock, Keeley was unable to keep her eyes open. Reminding her of a clucking Aunt Judith, Hazel escorted her to the spare bedroom and into bed. As she drifted into a deep sleep, she could still feel the imprint of Linc's soft mouth as it grazed her temple, and hear his whispered words in her ear, "Good-night, my darling, sleep well." *My darling,* she repeated in her groggy subconscious. They were such nice words. If only he meant them....

"Well, are you managing all right?" Linc inquired, glancing down at her from atop his magnificent animal. His grin was warm with concern as he took in the blushing pink in her cheeks and the sparkling brightness of her eyes.

"Oh, yes," she replied, a husky ripple in her voice. "And I'm sure I won't even be sore." She flashed him an impish grin, emphasizing her dimples.

"I wouldn't be too sure of that, if I were you." His eyes were full of devilment. "Although Jasper is a gentle lady, you're bound to feel the effects of not having ridden in a long time."

Some of the sparkle left her eyes. "I sure hope not," she said with pursed lips. "If I get too sore today, I won't be able to ride tomorrow." Her tone had a petulant ring to it.

"Don't worry. If it happens, I've got just the cure," Linc promised as he turned the reins of his horse to move closer to her mount. Both animals pranced side by side as they carried both riders across the irrigated pastures of Linc's land.

Keeley drew back and looked at him, a frown marring her features. "What cure?"

Linc's eyes danced merrily. "Somehow I get the

impression you don't trust me, Keeley Sanders. Am I right?''

"One hundred percent," she quipped as she shifted uncomfortably in the saddle.

Linc's loud infectious laughter caused both horses' ears to perk up, especially Jacob's, the sleek black animal that Linc had raised and trained from birth. They were a perfect match, Keeley observed with admiration. Arrogance and pride were the dominating forces in both the man and the beast. Keeley couldn't keep her eyes from straying to the boldness of his thighs as they strained against Jacob's wide flanks.

She whipped her head around, suddenly feeling overheated. What is there about this man, she wondered for the thousandth time, that makes me yearn with a deep-seated ache to know his touch? All of it. It was like she was being hit repeatedly by something hard and bruising only to find that the stroke felt light and not at all painful.

"What do you think of my empire?" Linc asked, breaking into her thoughts. "I couldn't wait until I had you all to myself, so I could show you every square inch of it." He smiled ruefully. "I love Hazel and Duffy dearly, but they have a tendency to smother me under their adoration."

Keeley laughed. "So I noticed."

"Huh!" His eyes narrowed lazily. "If I'm not mistaken, Hazel hovered over *you* like a clucking hen over her baby chicks, especially when she wouldn't let me anywhere near your room until noon today."

Keeley felt a blush creep up her cheeks. "I—I don't know what came over me," she said, an embarrassed tremor shaking her voice. "I've never in my whole life slept that long or that soundly, even when I was sick." There was a brief hesitation. "Maybe it was all the good food and wine we had last night, along with laughing at Duffy's outrageous stories, that made me sleep so well."

As they leisurely roamed over the graceful rolling hills, she felt an undeniable sense of peace steal over her. Although she knew this feeling wouldn't last, she nevertheless intended to enjoy every moment of it.

She had even managed to lock away all the guilt feelings concerning Jim, her father and her job. When she left this heavenly place, it would all come crashing down upon her head, but until that time, nothing would interfere with the contentment that weaved a spell around them. Abruptly their horses stopped in front of a cold stream that whistled its way through the silent hills.

Keeley watched as they lowered their heads and lapped thirstily at the cold spring water. She could hear the swish of their tails making a music all their own in the velvet silence of the late evening.

She ventured a tentative look in Linc's direction. He was watching her with eyes that glittered with suppressed fire.

Keeley felt her heart turn a double flip in her chest as his eyes continued to hold her captive. Suddenly he moved out of the saddle in a single coordinated motion and came around to help her dismount.

Linc's hand held hers in a tight grip as she struggled to maintain her balance.

"Oh—oh, me!" she groaned, reaching to clutch her backside. Her legs, too, threatened to crumble beneath her weight. "As much as I hate to admit it, you're right. I'm going to be stiff in the morning."

Her voice was a trifle unsteady as Linc's strong arm circled her waist.

"Didn't I tell you not to worry, that I have the perfect cure for what ails you?" His eyes were steaming dangerously as they peered down into her up-turned face.

"You—you—still haven't told me what your magic cure is yet," she voiced cautiously. "Anyway, I—I can feel the strength returning to my legs now," she assured him quickly.

She was extremely conscious of the heavy weight of his arm as it remained around her and the rumble of his laughter as it teased her ear. Damn! she thought. Why was it that he could always read her mind? She pointedly ignored him as she concentrated on the serenity of the mountains and the lower pastures in the distance, dotted with a large barn and a large riding ring. The touch of his fingers lingered and seemed to burn through her clothes to sear her sensitive skin. She could feel his body heat mixed with that of the horses to create an odor that was pleasant. It smelled like the man beside her—rough and untamed. She felt a raw ache spread throughout her body.

He laughed gently as his big hand moved from her waist down to caress the cheeks of her buttocks. "How about here, lovely Keeley?" he asked blatantly. "Can you deny it still smarts?"

Keeley placed her heart on idle as his hands erotically massaged the soreness from her body.

"If you think that feels good, just wait until you see what further healing powers I have in store for you," he promised, his tone low and silky smooth.

Keeley sensed immediately that he wasn't immune

to the havoc he was causing in her body. He, too, was feeling the harsh bite of unfulfilled passion. It showed in the jerky movement of his hand and in his sudden erratic breathing and flared nostrils.

The air around them crackled with emotional tension.

"Come on," Linc whispered unsteadily in her ear. "I've got something to show you." Removing his arm, he grasped her hand and drew her forward. "Think you're up to walking a little ways, or shall we try the horses again?" A soft grin lurked shamelessly in the corners of his mouth.

She moaned. "Forget the horses. I'll take my chances on walking. What do you have up your sleeve, Linc Hunter?" Her green eyes were wide with suspicion. "I trust you about as far as I can throw you."

A person could drown in those eyes, he thought as he noticed with covetous longing the fragile loveliness of her upturned face. Hungrily he devoured her. Without premeditation, he dipped his head and crushed her parted lips with the bold urgency of his own.

When Keeley felt the insistence of his sweet tongue, she moaned and reached up and locked her arms around his neck. They touched everywhere. Keeley felt as if her bones melted into him.

"God, Keeley," he groaned against her ravaged lips. "You taste so good, smell so good and feel so damn good." Then suddenly he pulled back. "If we don't move this instant, I'm liable to ravish you right here on the spot."

Taking him at his word, she scooted forward in spite of her sore muscles.

''Chicken,'' he murmured softly from close behind her as his long stride easily overtook her short one. His warm, unexpected breath against her ear caused a shiver to shoot through her.

For the next fifteen minutes they strolled in peaceful silence. Keeley didn't know how much longer she could continue to make her sore muscles respond, when they finally reached a clearing nestled among the thick pine thicket.

In front of her sat a small, austere cabin. Keeley turned toward Linc with questioning eyes. She didn't understand any of this. Suddenly her heart took a plunging dive. Surely he hadn't brought her here just to seduce her? Not like this! Premeditated! She clutched her hand against her stomach.

Seeing the dark expression cross her features, Linc uttered a savage oath. ''Damn it, Keeley, it's not what you think! Please, don't look at me like that.''

His words of reassurance had the desired effect. A warm smile broke across Keeley's face, replacing the horrified and pinched look of a moment ago. Her stance also relaxed. ''Then *why* did you bring me here?''

Linc smiled sheepishly and cocked his head in the direction of a small expanse of water next to the cabin. ''I thought you might enjoy a nice soothing dip in the hot spring.'' His eyes were dancing with mischief. ''It's guaranteed to cure all aches and pains.''

Seven

Keeley's head snapped back with a vengeance as she stared up at Linc, her eyes containing a strange mixture of fear and wanting.

"Well?"

"Well, what?" she asked breathlessly.

"Are you willing to let the hot spring get the crimp out of your weary muscles?" His eyes blazed over her face, challenging her.

Keeley turned her gaze away, fighting for control. How inviting the warm percolating water looked, she thought wistfully. She wanted to enjoy its soothing pleasure. Temptation loomed larger and larger.

Immediately her mind began to shout warnings, but it was an insignificant little voice, far away, and certainly no match for the desire that rushed through her body. Excitement followed as a reinforcement at the thought of having Linc's hands on her naked flesh. She was caught in a sensual web of her own making.

She bit down sharply on her lip to stop its trembling before she turned her eyes back to Linc.

He saw the battle racing within her. Her indecision was reflected in the rapid pulse beating at the base of her throat. His eyes pleaded with her to share this experience with him, to trust him. There was no need for words. His eyes mirrored all the same turbulent emotions that were quivering through her.

As if she were a robot, she extended a hand toward him. Quickly closing the gap between them, he reached out and enclosed her hand warmly within his.

"The towels—" He paused to clear his throat. "The clean towels are in the cabin."

The moment they entered the small and relatively bare living area, Keeley's teeth began to chatter. Her nerves were as tightly wound as a violin string. When Linc kicked the door shut she jumped as if she'd been shot.

What did he think of her? It was obvious that she was behaving very strangely. Can he possibly be nervous too? she wondered as she watched him move in the direction of the adjoining bathroom. Never removing her gaze from the coordinated strides of his muscular body, she took in the rather dilapidated-looking bed, the rickety bedside table and a kitchen table with two wooden straight-backed chairs. However, she noted with relief that it was meticulously clean. The floor as well as the spartan kitchen cabinet had been scrubbed so hard that the wood was a faded, washed-out brown.

Shortly Linc stepped out of the bathroom with two folded towels in his arms. "Here's your towel. You can change in there if you like." He inclined his head toward the bath.

Without speaking, she grabbed the towel, dashed quickly into the tiny room and slammed the door behind her. She leaned back against it as she struggled to regain her composure. She was behaving like a fugitive fleeing from the law.

Keeley took several deep breaths and then raced to

remove her clothes. Her task completed, she unfolded the fluffy towel, secured it tightly around her upper body and placed her hand firmly on the doorknob. Before advancing any farther, she glanced down to make sure the terry cloth adequately covered the private parts of her body.

Linc was standing there, waiting for her, his towel draped haphazardly around his tapered waist.

"I'm ready," she said in a voice that was slightly breathless from haste as well as from the powerful impact of seeing Linc's practically nude body, a bulwark, in front of her.

Suddenly, she had the urge to reach out and undo the towel which shielded the rest of his body from her eyes. She felt both feverish and greedy to know the surging boldness of his passion against the entire length of her soft, yielding limbs.

"Keeley, please, don't look at me like that," Linc pleaded harshly, shattering her erotic musings. "Damn! How much do you think a man can take?" he added, more to himself than to her.

Again she felt her face flush scarlet as she turned and hastily opened the cabin door. The crisp chilly air hit her partially unclad body with a bristling slap.

But her footsteps never faltered. She made her way toward the bubbling hot spring with the sole intention of getting in the water before Linc. Why was she behaving so erratically? It seemed as if she was split into a Dr. Jekyll and Mr. Hyde personality—one minute she was giving him a definite come-on and the next minute she was playing the outraged virgin.

"Keeley, wait…"

She froze abruptly in her tracks at the sound of his voice. It wasn't so much what he said but the way in which he said it. His tone was both demanding and persuasive.

"Please," he murmured from close behind her, "don't deny me the pleasure of seeing your body. It seems like I've waited for this moment all my life."

"Linc..."

"I only want to hold you.... Please, I know that's what you want too or you wouldn't be here with me now with nothing between us but a loose towel," he pleaded softly.

Taking her silence for acquiescence, he moved swiftly toward the spring. "I'll go first and test it." His tone was lighter, more confident. He sounded as if he had won the first round of a major skirmish.

Keeley's eyes remained glued to his back as he paused at the edge of the pool with deliberate thoroughness and unhitched the towel, flinging it swiftly to the side. Exposed to her full vision was the wide expanse of his shoulders, rippling with muscles that looked to be made of steel. Next, her eyes were privy to his waist that nipped in just enough on each side to proportion him evenly.

Then her eyes hungrily sought and found the roundness of his buttocks, softer and lighter in color than the rest of his body. Her heart tilted and then took a nose dive, landing with a thud in her churning stomach as her eyes memorized the smooth hardness of those manly cheeks. With her tongue stuck to the dry roof of her mouth, she longed to touch, to knead this tender portion of his body and bring him to the peak of deep and fulfilling passion.

She couldn't move or speak. It was as if her limbs were made of liquid putty. She was powerless to help herself as she watched Linc's big bare body hit the pool.

The splash of the warm water on her face brought her out of her stupor. She stared at him.

"Keeley, I'm waiting," Linc urged, a sweet smile pushing his lips upward. "This has got to be the greatest feeling in the whole world." His eyes never veered from her face. They burned brightly with both happiness and desire as they pleaded with her to join him.

Suddenly, Keeley felt her body reel with shock as the seriousness of the situation came crashing down upon her. *What am I doing? It's wrong! I know it's wrong!* She was trembling. Her brain kept shouting, *Run! Run!* but her body was insisting, *Stay! Stay!*

"Keeley..." His voice and hand beckoned to her.

Then, as if her body and her mind were two separate entities, she slowly unclasped the towel and watched it fall gracefully from her body.

The sharp intake of Linc's breath vibrated through the tall pines, bringing the birds' chirpy voices to a sudden halt. Every soft curve of her body was seared into Linc's brain as his eyes plundered her at will.

He reached up and clasped her hand tightly within his and slowly pulled her downward into the warm water. Linc then backed away and let his eyes feast on the rounded curves of her sweet breasts as the tingling liquid swirled gently around them.

"Well, how do you like it so far?" Linc asked. "Can you feel the heat working on your sore muscles?"

Keeley giggled. "It feels absolutely marvelous! I can't believe what I've been missing out on all these years!" Impulsively she flung her arms around Linc who now stood directly in front of her. "Oh, thank you! Thank you! Thank you!"

"You're more than welcome," he murmured, his eyes turning to hot points of passion as her jutting breasts grazed against his chest.

Suddenly everything changed. The merriment between them ceased. Keeley's breath lay paralyzed in her throat as Linc lowered his mouth to cover hers. She opened her mouth to him and for a long, sweet moment their tongues met. He pulled back and looked at her with raw hunger in his eyes.

"Do I have your permission to make your sore body well?" he asked, in a voice throbbing with longing.

She nodded mutely, too weak to answer as he continued his assault on her senses. His lips nibbled at the sensitive spot on her neck before moving slowly back up to tickle her ear with his hot tongue.

"Linc," she whispered weakly.

Then she felt his hands as they began a sensual journey down her body, seeking, touching, probing until they reached the rounded cheeks of her buttocks. He then gently lifted her upward until she was able to lock her legs around his upper thighs.

Her breasts with their tilted nipples lapped against his chest as he began slowly massaging her abused lower body.

Keeley felt she was dying a slow death as his fingers pushed and delved and circled the tender skin. Every nerve ending in her body quivered as she gave herself up to this erotic manipulation of her flesh.

Linc was aware of a growing tightness in his chest as he continued to worship this lovely creature in his arms. He was keenly aware of everything about her;

all of his five senses were working overtime as they enjoyed her sweet curves, her warmth, her softness, the clean scent of her flesh with its lingering trace of perfume.

"Keeley, God! I want you so desperately!" he groaned against her lips. "I think I may die from wanting you."

From the far reaches of her mind, Keeley responded to his plea. Her finger touched his eyes with fluttering gentleness before moving to trace the inner moistness of his lips. "I want you too," she murmured, her voice barely above a whisper.

But Linc was powerless to move, to take what she was so sweetly offering him, for her fingers that he so well remembered were now roaming his upper body, concentrating with eagerness on the diamond hardness of his tiny breasts nestled so proudly within the wiry mat that covered his chest.

Before he realized it, Keeley had loosened her legs from around his body and was now standing apart from him. Her hands began wandering lower to the flat planes of his stomach. Immediately she felt him tense beneath her fingers as they teased his navel.

As she ventured lower, plunging him into deeper silent agony, Linc fought to get even. He reached out and cupped her breasts, filling his large hands with them as the hiss and patter of the gurgling water surged around their bodies. He dipped his head and took a turgid nipple between his teeth.

Even though Linc's mouth felt like tongues of fire on her skin, she remained true to her course. She didn't waver. The insistent hardness of his body reveled in the circling quest of her fingers.

A low groan began in the back of Linc's throat and finally erupted through his lips.

"Keeley, Keeley," he said as he stilled her hand, "this is madness. It's got to stop before it's too late."

"Linc—please—love me," she whispered achingly.

As the words connected with Linc's drugged brain the blood began to pound in his head with the force of a hammer. Was he dreaming? He couldn't be, not when she stood before him with her eyes aglow with passion.

"Linc—?"

Needing no further encouragement, Linc lifted her into his arms as if she were a precious newborn baby and covered quickly the short distance between the hot spring and the cabin. By now the temperature had dropped considerably. Away from the warm water, the air was bitingly cold. It nipped at their naked flesh, causing their teeth to chatter. The dilapidated cabin seemed like heaven as Linc pushed the door open with his foot and carried her across the room to the bed.

Laying her carefully upon it, he reached for the quilt that was folded neatly across the foot and covered her. He then leaned down and kissed her deeply before crossing the room to kneel down in front of the fireplace.

"Linc, what—?" Keeley began, bereaved at being left alone for even a moment. Then she felt her face flush hot with color as she wondered if that shaky, cracked sound had actually come from her throat.

He turned immediately and looked at her, a slow smile warming his face. "I'll only be a minute, love," he stated huskily. "I felt we would be much more comfortable with a little heat in this airy place."

Keeley watched as he picked up a couple of pieces of dried wood that rested upon the brick hearth and stacked them behind the old beat-up set of andirons. Then, with little effort of his part, he soon had a small but glowing fire lit in the fireplace.

As he stood in hesitation for one brief moment, making sure it would continue to burn, Keeley once more treated herself to another perusal of his beautiful body. As the firelight danced around him, it showed every delightful contour of his physique to perfection. Such a lean, hard man, she thought, but at the same time so gentle and unselfish in his ability to give.

Suddenly as he made his way across the room and came to stand beside the bed, she realized that she wanted Linc Hunter with every ounce of energy that pulsated through her body. *Love?* Of course not! *Want?* Yes.

Along with this burst of knowledge came the awesome burden that it placed upon her heart. Was this moment of passion worth it? Was it? Her heart was weeping as the springs squeaked and the mattress sagged from the weight of Linc's body.

Then the tears began to flow from her eyes as Linc pitched back the cover and stretched his long frame out beside her.

"Keeley, darling, what's the matter?" he groaned as he gently folded her into his arms. "Surely you know by now that I wouldn't hurt you for anything in the world." His fingers traveled to smooth away the straying tendrils that clung to her dampened cheeks. "Shh, don't cry—please, I promise not to do anything. Please, tell me what's wrong." His voice had grown agonizingly raw as he continued to clutch her tightly against him.

She pulled back as far as his arms would let her and raised tear-stained eyes to his face. "Nothing— nothing's wrong," she gulped between the sobs that crowded her throat, "Just—just love me. *Now!*" *Before it's too late,* her inner mind cried. *For us, there is no tomorrow.*

"Yes, oh, yes," Linc moaned against her mouth as his hands began to explore her body. Slowly, slowly, he moved his fingers down the inside of her gorgeous legs, so open to him in the muted glow of the crackling firelight. On reaching her fragile ankles, his fingers journeyed back up her limbs. Even her calves weren't slighted in this pilgrimage to reach her shapely thighs and then finally home to the womanly part of her that held his very soul. There he lingered in mindless joy until the thrashing groan of her body told him that she was utterly fulfilled.

Linc felt as if he was hooked on some new and exotic drug as he moved upward to knead the taut flesh of her breasts. While his finger teased one, his mouth clung to and teased the other.

Keeley's hands roamed over him too, stroking and squeezing his hard muscles, and her fingers teased his face, head and temple until she finally drew his lips away from her breasts. She kissed the corners of his mouth, until he sought greedily the full pressure of hers.

Immediately they were swamped in sensations that neither had felt before as their tongues intertwined and the kiss became hot, fiercely hot, and liquid.

"Oh, sweet Keeley," he uttered as he drew his lips from hers, "you have no concept of how I've ached to hold you like this, with nothing between us but the air we breathe.''

"I know," she whispered as she boldly nipped at his lips with her mouth and teeth. Then she felt a tremble thunder through him when her fingers danced across his skin like tiny prickles of hot coals and encountered the huge steeliness of his desire and the intense heat that surrounded it.

Her gentle hands drove him wild. Her touch made him want to taste and memorize every delicious inch of her. And he proceeded to do just that.

She began to moan under the loving lash of his tongue.

"Linc!"

"Now, Keeley?" Linc urged. "Take me in!"

"Yes," she cried against his chest as his body moved to yield a gentle cover for her own. Then with sweet, bursting intensity she lured him into her fragrant passage, meshing them together as one.

She was breathing deeply, rapidly, as they moved in a rhythm as old as time. Every nerve ending in her body began to tingle as they reached the shattering finality. She was sure she would disintegrate into quivering bits and pieces.

For Linc, it had never been sweeter, and he knew with aching certainty that he would never be able to let her go.

Afterward they remained side by side as their heartbeats slowly gentled.

Keeley was both mentally and physically exhausted, but she couldn't sleep. Her mind was obsessed with thoughts of Linc and the intense pleasure that he'd given her. It was not just sexual fulfillment, although that was indescribably thrilling and something she had never experienced. It was something more, something new to her, something precious and powerful that went beyond words.

Had Linc felt it too? she wondered. Could he possibly care more than she knew? Was she perhaps more than a passing fancy to him, more than just a warm body? Maybe the reason he ignored all pleas to discuss or sign his contract was because he meant to give up football? For her? *Don't be stupid,* she ridiculed herself. There had been nothing said about any commitment or love in the bargain. *Go to sleep. You're chasing rainbows that don't exist.*

Keeley stirred beneath the heavy weight of the blanket. What had awakened her? Was it the slam of a door? she questioned in confusion. Slowly, she forced her sagging eyelids open, becoming aware of the hazy daylight pouring through the window.

Her confusion mounted as her gaze focused on the raw dark wood that surrounded her. Then her eyes darted in several different directions at once. The instant Linc filled her vision, they widened in shocked dismay. Suddenly the events of last evening washed over her. She held her breath until she felt crazed for air as Linc, bare to the waist, was stacking several logs against the wall.

It seemed as though he felt the silent intensity of her gaze, for suddenly he whirled around and looked at her. Their eyes met and held. Slowly, an enduring smile covered his lips before traveling up to fill his eyes, turning them a sparkling blue.

"Good morning, sleepyhead," he said. "I was beginning to think I was going to have to tickle your toes in order to wake you up!"

Color dotted both cheeks as she fought to come to grips with what had taken place between them. As her eyes raked over him, beginning with the top of his damp unruly hair down to the jeans that slung low on his hips, she realized with a burst of happiness that last night hadn't been a dream. Every heart-throbbing moment they shared had been wonderfully, gloriously *real!*

She felt a sense of giddy well-being and anticipation course through her body as Linc strolled over to the bed and leaned over her. He was so close now that she could almost taste the minty smell of his breath and count the tiny lines that nestled in the corner of his eyes.

"Do you have any idea how happy you've made me?" he asked deeply. "My life took on new meaning the moment my body joined with yours. I felt I had truly come home."

Suddenly her face clouded. "Oh, Linc, I wish—" she began.

"Shhh," he demanded, placing his fingers abruptly against her lips. "Don't say anything. No recriminations, no apologies, no soul-searching. Nothing. For now it's only the two of us basking in the magic we've created. Agreed?"

Her features cleared and she flashed him a tumultuous smile, then scooted over, making room for him on the bed.

As he lowered his bulky frame down beside her, he found himself imprinting on his mind the image of her loveliness as she clutched the blanket around her bare breasts. Her hair hung in a beautiful disarray about her shoulders. Suddenly, she moved her head, causing an errant strand to brush across his face like a whisper in the wind. This innocent action had the power to make him grow with longing.

He tried to speak, to tell her that he was falling in love with her, but he was afraid of driving a wedge further between them. He knew that she was still fighting her past and clinging to dreams of a perfect future with a man she didn't love. She was still afraid to take a chance; he was not without uncertainties either. Admitting that he loved her would be no easy task for him. He had never spoken those words to any woman, except his mother. So what if they each had their own private shadows that must be brought to light and worked out? It didn't matter. Nothing mattered now except his hungry, excruciating need for her.

He bent his head and kissed her moist, parted lips and then, tenderly, nibbled on the soft curve of her breast.

"How do you feel now, this minute?" he asked slowly, reverently. "Be honest."

Keeley drew back and looked at him. "Mmmm," she said, stretching lazily. "I feel like a million dollars."

He grinned. "Are you sure you're all right? It wasn't too much?" Concern suddenly wiped the grin from his lips.

She broke into a wide smile. "No, although it's been so—so long. You were perfect, and I—"

His lips stopped her. He crushed her against him with a feeling akin to desperation. When he finally released her, there was an unspoken question in his eyes.

"Keeley?"

"Please."

"Are you sure?"

"Today. Now. My body belongs to you," she whispered. She touched his face with trembling fingers.

"Magic," he breathed on a last desperate note before gently lowering her once again into the sagging softness of the bed.

Keeley felt her flesh come alive and then melt against Linc as he began a replay of their passion-filled night. In a few precious moments, Linc gave her enough beautiful memories to last her a lifetime and beyond.

"Thank God, you're back!" a harassed Hazel shouted at them as they reined their mounts to a stop. Her features were pinched, making her look old and worn.

"What the hell?" Linc began as Hazel grabbed hold of Keeley's bridle and stared up at her.

Keeley's heart plummeted to her toes and a chill spread throughout her body. She stared at Hazel mutely.

"Keeley, honey," Hazel said, her tone somewhat softer now, "the phone's been ringing off the wall for you since early this morning." Keeley's gasp did nothing to halt her words. "In fact, the same party's holding for you right now," she finished on a shrill note. "You'd best hurry, I fear it's bad news."

"Damn it, Hazel! Don't scare the girl out of her wits until we have all the facts," Linc demanded harshly. He then dismounted with pantherlike grace and covered the distance between him and Keeley. Reaching up, he took her hand and helped her down.

Paralysis held her in its grip with hands of iron.

But once she felt the solid ground beneath her, she felt a surge of energy return to her stunned limbs.

With an anguished cry erupting from her lips, she broke away from Linc's restraining hand and charged into the house. Frantically she searched the living room until she found the phone. For an instant she stared at it and cringed. It was as if it were a poisonous snake, coiled, just waiting to spring.

When she finally placed it against her ear, her voice was barely audible. "Hello—"

"Thank God," Jim replied, his usually calm voice now sounding rattled and grim. "Where the hell have you been? Because of what you've done your father is lying here in the hospital in intensive care. And where are you? You're off gallivanting with some jock—"

"No! No! No!" Keeley whimpered as her bubble of happiness shattered into a million pieces, covering her in staggering force with guilt, fright and panic.

Unable to bear the burden, she clawed at the air around her for support before unconsciousness overtook her.

Eight

The clinical smell of the hospital swamped Keeley's senses the minute she scurried through the swinging doors, and the spotless white walls seemed to close in on her as she made her way toward the elevator. Even Linc's hand, firmly planted at the bend of her elbow, failed to ward off the impending threat of doom that hung over her like a black thundercloud.

Although she tried to persuade Linc not to come with her, he was insistent and determined. Far too shaken and upset to fight him, Keeley had acquiesced, but with the understanding that he would escort her to the door of the cardiac intensive care unit and no further. With a tightening of his jaw and a hard glint in his eye he had agreed.

She would have it no other way.

Her life had been a horror-filled nightmare from the moment Linc had revived her with a cold sponge and sip of brandy. As quickly as possible, she had changed her clothes and then Linc, at breakneck speed, had driven them to the airport.

During the entire time that they had swept through the sun-blistering sky toward Portland, a feeling of self-loathing had thrummed inside her skull. She had let her dreams get in the way of her sound judgment, she told herself in weary disillusionment. For what?

A night in the arms of a man who had no intention of offering her anything permanent.

Now as they waited for the elevator Linc turned toward her and announced grimly, "Keeley, I have no intention of leaving you here."

"You promised," she said dully.

He stifled a curse. "No, I didn't!"

"Yes, you did. I heard you."

"Damn it, Keeley," he began, only to clamp his jaws together, cutting off his words altogether. He took a deep breath and patiently tried another approach. "Let me put it this way, I don't *want* to leave you. You need me!"

"No, no, I don't need you," she lied. Her voice sounded foreign, even to her own ears.

Linc felt a rising sense of frustration as he tried to get through to her. Hell! He cursed inwardly, it wouldn't do for him to get a hold of that man she called her fiancé. He was sorely afraid he'd be hard pressed not to put his fist through his face. By the time he'd revived Keeley the phone on the other end was dead. But he had managed to pry out of Keeley, bit by bit, the gist of what he'd said to her. How she could even contemplate marrying that sniveling pencil pusher was beyond him.

"What on earth is wrong with the elevator?" Her voice cracked on a sob as she jammed the red button several times. "I can't imagine what's taking it so long. The stairs. Where are the stairs?" She whirled around and began searching frantically for the exit sign.

Keeley's sudden movement brought Linc out of his moody thoughts. He laid a restraining hand on her arm but didn't have to enforce it. The elevator clanged and the doors slid back gracefully.

A weary but calm Judith was the first person Keeley saw as she rounded the corner placing her on the fourth-floor cardiac wing. Judith stood outside the door deep in conversation with a nurse.

Seeing Keeley, she excused herself with a bleak smile and made her way toward her. Keeley practically ran headlong into her aunt's outstretched arms. They held each other close for a long moment before breaking apart.

Linc refused to disappear altogether, but faded into the background as much as possible. The grief between the two women was almost tangible as they comforted each other. He was determined to remain close just in case Keeley needed him.

"How is he?" Keeley asked in a strangled voice.

Judith shook her head. "Not good, I'm afraid."

Keeley stifled a sob. "When—when can I see him?"

"There's not another visitation time for thirty more minutes," Judith replied, chewing on her lower lip.

Keeley saw the dark rings around her aunt's eyes and the added wrinkles to her beautiful skin. She felt her heart almost burst under the weary load she carried.

"Aunt Judith," Keeley said, "I'm so sorry, so sorry." Tears welled up in her eyes and slowly trickled down her face. She groped for a tissue from her purse and dabbed at her eyes. "Please, what happened? Tell me. Every detail." The tears were pouring profusely as she reached for another tissue. "How did Dad find out where I was?"

Judith's shoulders sagged. "There's a waiting room

that joins the unit. Why don't we sit in there and talk? By the way, Jim is here," she volunteered almost as an afterthought. She saw Keeley's face drain of the rest of its color but continued. "He left just a few minutes before you arrived to get himself something to eat and bring me back a cup of coffee. I—" Judith stopped and stared beyond Keeley's right shoulder.

Keeley knew without turning around that Judith had seen Linc. Suddenly, she felt his presence behind her. She longed to rest her tired body against his strong, healthy one and let him hold her and comfort her. But that crazy thought didn't last long. She bounced back to reality with a jolt. *Linc must leave before Jim returned.* She couldn't cope with a confrontation between the two of them.

With a slight nod in Linc's direction, Judith said in a cold voice, "Keeley, I'll wait for you in the room. Don't be long."

Keeley nodded mutely before turning around to face Linc. She noticed that his eyes were also cold and hard, and his breathing uneven, as he watched Judith's disappearing back.

"Well, I've certainly been put in my place," he stated emphatically. "I gather that I'm to blame."

Keeley's insides shook. "No, don't think that any of this mess is your fault. It all rests squarely upon my shoulders. I should never have sneaked off with you for the weekend like a star-struck teenager. I'm a grown woman with responsibilities—a fiancé for starters—and what I did was wrong—"

Linc's nostrils flared and fire shot from his eyes. "Don't you dare turn what we shared into something evil," he hissed in a low voice. "You may have a verbal agreement with what's-his-face, but by God he doesn't own you yet."

Suddenly Keeley felt as if she were on public display as she saw several passersby give her and Linc strange looks. The last thing she needed was to create a scene in the middle of the hospital corridor.

"Linc, please. Don't do this. Not now. I've got to go. Aunt Judith needs me."

"And you don't think I do," he muttered harshly.

"Linc!"

He expelled his breath on a ragged note. "All right, I'll go. I'll be at my apartment if you need me." He paused and looked at her, without saying a word. Keeley felt herself begin to squirm under his intent gaze. "Just remember, you can shift all the blame to me—that's really where it belongs."

Keeley lowered her eyes, fanning her thick lashes against her cheeks as she groped blindly to get control of her emotions. When she looked up she saw Linc's retreating frame. Why did she suddenly feel as if part of her had gone with him?

Although the family waiting room was large, Keeley found Judith alone in the room. She crossed the room and sat down beside her on the small couch.

Coming straight to the point, she said, "Please, Aunt Judith, tell me what happened. What are Dad's chances?"

Judith's eyes were troubled, though she smiled briefly. "Just one question at a time, my dear." She sighed and looked as if she were searching for a way to begin. "Actually, the trouble started when Luther overheard a conversation in the training room the day before you left to go with Linc."

"*What!*"

"You heard me right," Judith replied without flinching.

"But—I—I don't understand?"

"From what I pieced together, your father heard several players laughing and making snide remarks about you and Linc."

"What was said?" Keeley asked in a low, strained tone.

Judith paled. "What difference could it possibly make now?"

"Tell me," Keeley insisted, her chin locked, stubbornly.

Judith's mouth slid into a straight line. "All right, have it your own way." She paused and averted her eyes. "I believe the comment went like this and I quote: 'You know Hunter will get what he wants. The sky's the limit. After all, he's laying the boss's daughter.'" Her face was beet red by the time she had finished speaking and turned her eyes back toward Keeley.

A whimper tore through Keeley as she slumped forward and put her head down into her hand. "Oh, no! No!" she muttered as a sob shook her entire body.

Although Judith placed a comforting hand on Keeley's back, she went on, her voice filled with intense and sympathetic pain. "Thursday afternoon and all day Friday, he ranted and raved like a man possessed. Then late Saturday he got word that Linc had gone to his ranch. When you were nowhere to be found, he put two and two together. All hell must have broken loose." There was a long pause while she struggled for control. "Early this morning he had his severe attack. His heart evidently couldn't handle the strain. Now all we can do is wait." Her lower lip quivered as she found and grasped Keeley's hand tight within her own.

"Oh, Aunt Judith," Keeley sobbed, the tears pouring out of her eyes onto their clasped hands. "I didn't mean to—"

"I know, I know," Judith interrupted in a soothing voice. "I'm sure you did what you thought you had to do. Only you know how much Luther was counting on you marrying Jim and settling down." She paused briefly. "And then to hear your name slurred like that on top of finding out that you'd been seeing Linc was just too much."

Keeley raised her glazed, pleading eyes up to Judith. "I wanted to tell him, so many times, but I just couldn't. I—I kept thinking I'd get Linc out of my system, but every time I was around him I just got in deeper until—until I was just like putty in his hands."

Judith released Keeley's hands and stood up and crossed wearily to the window, where she peered out at the busy freeway below. "Keeley, darling, I'm not going to sit in judgment and condemn you for what you've done," she said softly. "I'm not without my own share of guilt in all of this. Your father and I hadn't been getting along. He knew something was wrong with me, but I—I couldn't bear to tell him that I was going to marry someone else. So we just kept drifting further and further apart." She shrugged and bit her lip to keep it from trembling. "If only I'd been with him last night, maybe I could have calmed him down—smoothed things over a little." She rolled her fist into a ball. "Now I feel so useless," she added unhappily.

Keeley rose and quickly covered the distance between them. She placed her arm around Judith and leaned her head on her shoulder. "When—when Dad gets well, we'll both have to do better, won't we?" She raised her head and smiled through her tears. "Somehow I know, I can feel it here," she paused and laid a hand across her heart, "that Dad is going to come out of this attack just as he did all the others and give his favorite girls another chance."

Suddenly Judith wrapped her arms around Keeley and said on a desperate note, "I hope so, oh, God, I hope so."

Keeley pulled back. "Does that mean you aren't going to leave Dad and marry that—that other man?"

Judith moved back to the couch and sat down. "If your father will have me, I'll never leave him again, I promise," she stated softly but with a thread of iron underlying her every word.

There was nothing else to say following Judith's heart-rending vow. Keeley wearily rubbed the back of her neck and stretched her muscles. When she was straight once again, her expression froze.

Jim was standing in the door, eyeing her intently. Their eyes met for a brief moment before a shutter seemed to fall across his. Keeley had no idea what he was thinking as he made his way toward her. He stopped in front of her but made no effort to touch her. There was an awkward moment between them as they both searched for something to say.

Stuffing his hands down into his pockets and then bringing them out, showing his agitation, Jim finally said, "I'm sorry, Keeley. Can you ever forgive me for what I said and did to you?"

Keeley tried to force the tightness from her lips. "I'm—I'm the one who should be asking your forgiveness. I—"

"Don't say anything further." A ghost of a smile crossed his lips. "I'm prepared to forget it, if you are." Then suddenly his smile disappeared and his eyes narrowed. "That is, if you can promise me that nothing like that will ever happen again."

Keeley felt intense heat blister her cheeks as anger pounded through her body. God! How magnanimous can one get? she asked herself. Then immediately she regretted her thoughts. After all, he *was* giving her a second chance, which was more than most men would do. Anyway, this was not the time to discuss her and Jim's relationship.

Jim knew her well enough to realize that he'd said the wrong thing. A gut feeling told him that he was about to lose Keeley, and he couldn't bear to do that—at least not without a fight.

"Keeley—" He hesitated, an uncomfortable flush stealing up his face. "I—I don't always say things the right way." He swallowed. "What I meant to say was that I love you and don't want to lose you. And that I don't know what went wrong." He paused and nervously drew a cigarette from his shirt pocket and lit it. "But whatever it was," he rushed on, "I'm willing to try and make it right on my part. Just remember I love you and want to marry you."

Keeley no longer felt anger or anything close to it. What she did feel was torn—torn between three people who were all vying for part of her. It was tearing her up inside to be pulled in so many different directions at once. But now was not the time to be concerned about herself. Certainly not with her father's life hanging in the balance just a few steps away. For the time being, that took precedence over everything else. Her feelings could wait.

Her eyes were full of anguish as she raised them to Jim. "Please, I'm so upset about Dad I can't even think straight." She reached out and tentatively touched his face. He was good, kind and forgiving. Why couldn't she love him? Why couldn't he make her heart pound like—*Stop it, Keeley! Don't think about him!*

Jim clamped her hand against his cheek and then brought it around and touched the palm with his mouth. "Oh, Keeley, I do love you," he stressed as he continued to caress her palm.

Nothing. She felt nothing. His touch meant no more to her than her father's. It isn't fair, she moaned inwardly, it just isn't fair. But she had to try to love him—it was the only way.

"Will you sit with me and Aunt Judith?"

Jim's face brightened with relief. "Of course, you know I will," he promised in a soft voice. "We'll see this thing through together—all of us."

Judith joined them once they were seated on the couch. While Jim took the lid off Judith's coffee and added the cream and sugar to it Keeley turned and faced her aunt.

"You never did finish telling me the details of Dad's attack," Keeley said quietly.

Judith reached for her coffee and took a sip before answering. "It was a horrible evening, as I've already mentioned to you. He was like a madman, uncontrollable. But to make a long story short, I finally exacted a promise from him to go to bed and try to get some sleep and that we would talk some more the following day." Suddenly tears sprang up in her eyes again. "I—I never should have left him," she wailed. She paused a moment to get control of herself before continuing. "The—the next morning Jim called and broke the news to me."

"Jim called you!" Keeley parroted, making no attempt to hide her shock and dismay.

"Yes, Jim," Judith explained patiently. "Apparently he'd just arrived at Luther's looking for you when Joseph was frantically calling for an ambulance." She paused and looked at Jim for confirmation and help.

"After that," Jim chimed in, "I immediately called Judith and she met us at the hospital." He paused and took a deep breath. "The rest you know."

For a moment there was a heavy silence in the room as they sat and watched the evening shadows begin to sneak through the windows.

Then suddenly the swinging door into the waiting room opened and Dr. Willis came striding through it. Keeley jumped up and rushed toward him. A sharp pain jabbed at her chest.

"Daddy's not—not going to die, is he?" she asked in an unsteady voice.

He hesitated a moment, then shook his head. "I don't know, Keeley. I honestly don't know."

"Please," she pressed, "Isn't there anything you can do?"

He sighed deeply as he adjusted the stethoscope around his neck. "Not at the moment, my dear. We're doing all that's humanly possible for Luther." He looked at her kindly from under white bushy eyebrows. "But you don't need to be told that, do you? Luther is more than a patient; he's a friend."

Keeley squeezed his hand before letting it go. "I—I know," she gulped. "It—it's just that I'm so afraid.'' Her voice had dropped to an agonizing whisper.

"I'll let you know the moment there's a change.''

"When can I see him?''

Dr. Willis shook his head. "He's resting comfortably now. Although technically you're allowed to see him for ten minutes every so often, I'm going to forfeit that privilege right now."

Keeley opened her mouth as if to object and then closed it firmly when she saw the stubborn look that appeared on his face.

"I don't want anything to disturb him, now. Nothing at all." In spite of his abrupt manner, his eyes poured sympathy and concern. "There's a nurse monitoring his condition continuously. I'll keep you posted." After a nod in Judith's and Jim's direction, he quickly took his leave, his steps brisk and confident.

There was nothing left to do but wait. And wait they did. Jim tried to get Keeley to let him get her something to eat, but she refused. Though she consumed more hot, black coffee than she cared to admit.

Finally, around twelve o'clock, Dr. Willis emerged through the swinging doors once again. Keeley sat petrified as he came toward her. She was too tired and worried to move. She waited.

"It's another miracle," he said to all of them with the threat of a smile curving his lips, "but Luther's condition has stabilized. However," he went on hurriedly, "it's much too soon to assess the extent of the damage. That will come later."

"Oh, thank you, thank you, doctor," Keeley cried, her eyes brimming with tears.

"My advice is for all of you to go home now and get some rest and come back early in the morning."

Jim drove Keeley and Judith home. Keeley tried to persuade him to remain at her apartment and sleep on the couch, but he refused. He was afraid she wouldn't rest as well, so he insisted upon returning to his room at the motel.

Keeley felt terrible that she couldn't convince him to stay, but when she saw that he was adamant, she gave up. He left with a promise to meet her at the hospital in the morning.

After a hot shower, Keeley lay in bed and stared up at the ceiling. Her eyes felt as if they were full of grit; they burned and itched, keeping her from closing them. After getting up and doctoring them with eye-drops she lay back down, but still sleep remained an elusive prey.

Her thoughts centered on her father and the jumbled-up mess she'd made of her life. She rolled over with a groan and punched the pillow several times in hopes of shutting out visions of what her father's face must have looked like when he heard that nasty comment. Also she kept recalling the harsh and angry words Jim had spoken to her on the phone. And then there was Linc. Oh, God, how she wanted and needed him. Even when she knew it was so wrong. She hated herself for thinking about him, for letting thoughts of him control not only her mind but also her body as well.

Finally, after raking sobs tore through her, she was able to plunge her mind into a deep void and sleep.

When she arrived at the hospital the next morning, Judith was already there. Keeley learned from the

nurse on duty that Dr. Willis had allowed Judith to
see her father for a brief moment.

She felt somewhat encouraged by the fact that Luther was able to have visitors. It appeared that his
condition must have remained stable throughout the
long night.

But when Judith came out into the waiting room
five minutes later her face was grave.

"Aunt Judith?" Keeley gasped as she stood up and
clutched a hand to her heart. "Has he—?"

Judith's face cleared a little on seeing Keeley's face
turn tissue-paper white. "No." She sighed, slinging
her handbag on the couch beside Keeley before sitting
down beside her. "Actually he's better this morning."

Keeley wasn't convinced. There was something
wrong. She could feel the bad vibrations in her bones.

"If—if he's better, Aunt Judith, then why the long
and glum face?"

A deep silence fell between them.

"I want to see him," Keeley announced abruptly
as she jumped up from the couch and headed for the
door. Fear had wrapped its tentacles around her heart
and was squeezing it hard and tight.

"No—wait, Keeley. Please—" Judith begged as
she followed her to the door. "You can't!"

Keeley whirled around on the balls of her feet. Her
eyes were flashing wildly. "Can't what?" she demanded.

Judith slumped against the door in front of her and
looked at Keeley with agony in her eyes. "Your—
your father refuses to see you. He—"

Keeley stood still. Motionless. She had the sensation of having been kicked in the stomach. Then an-

ger, sorrow and disillusionment overcame her until she could think no more.

"Keeley, honey," Judith pleaded as she took Keeley's cold hands in her warm ones and began rubbing them in a soothing motion, "he just needs time, that's all, just time. You must try to understand—"

Keeley raised her hand and stopped Judith's gentle flow of words. "It's all right—really it is. I understand," she whispered stoically, "but I'm going home now." She caught back a sob. "Promise me you'll stay and look after him."

Judith leaned over and kissed her on the cheek. "You know I will," she said. "I love him with my life." Her voice broke and she looked away.

Keeley turned after opening the door and stepping into the hall. "Please tell Jim that I'll call him later. That I—I don't want to be disturbed."

She had never felt so alone or frightened in her life, not even when she was a small child vying for her father's affection, as she did now. As the steel door of the hospital zipped closed behind her, she prayed that she would be able to make peace with her father before it was too late.

Keeley woke up with a start. The loud bam! bam! bam! ringing in her ear stirred her into action. She flung back the covers on the bed and raced into the living room.

Being awakened by someone beating on her door was getting to be a habit, she thought with vexation.

"Jim? Is that you?" she called as she fumbled with the tie on her robe.

The door handle continued to rattle, grating against

her befuddled senses like fingernails scraping against
a chalkboard. She cringed.

"Keeley, it's me. Open the door." The pace of her
heart quickened even more as she recognized the
voice.

Complying with his demand, she swung the door
wide on its hinges. The sudden chill of the late evening air hit her square in the face as she stepped aside
for Linc to enter.

Closing the door quickly, she turned and followed
him into the room. Another chill shook her body,
causing her to move in the direction of the central
heat control on the wall. After adjusting it to a higher
temperature, she turned to confront Linc.

His expression told her that he was well aware that
her day had been hell. Compassion and another emotion equally as potent poured from his eyes as he
strode toward her. He stopped short of touching her,
jamming his hands in his pockets instead.

"How's Luther?" he asked.

"Better." She averted her eyes. "He's—he's stable, holding his own."

Keeley heard his thankful sigh as he reached out a
hand and cupped her chin, turning her to face him.

Keeley felt a quiver jerk through her and closed
her eyes. She prayed that God would forgive her for
wanting Linc. She wanted him to hold her and love
her. She needed him so.

"Then why the long face and tear-stained cheeks?"
he questioned, breaking into her fragmented thoughts.

His gentleness was Keeley's undoing. She felt her
insides heave and then crumble. She burst into tears.

Linc hauled her into his arms with a groan, pressing
her face against his chest. He held her close and

rocked her like a baby, trying to calm her down with sweet and comforting words.

When the tears were finally spent, Linc led her over to the couch. After they were seated, he cradled her within his strong arms again. She snuggled up to him like a homing pigeon to its nest, letting his strength fill her with a warm sense of belonging.

"Tell me about it," he prodded softly.

Between gulps all the sordid facts unfolded. She repeated word for word the conversation between her and Judith concerning the degrading and snide remarks overheard by her father at the gym, followed by the painful news of her father's refusal to see her. The whole time she talked, Linc stroked her hair, her back and neck, hoping she would relax in his arms, but her muscles remained tense and unyielding.

"Do you think he'll ever forgive me?" she asked, looking up at him in search of reassurance.

His chiseled lips narrowed into a thin line. "Keeley, I want you to listen to me for a moment," he stressed. "You've done nothing to ask forgiveness for."

"Oh, but—" Her lower lip quivered.

"Don't interrupt. Let me finish. What we've shared together wasn't wrong, isn't wrong. Maybe the way in which we went about it wasn't one hundred percent on the up and up." He shrugged. "But you're a grown woman, no longer Daddy's little girl who must do everything to please him. Nor should you have to account to him for your time."

Keeley's eyes widened as she suddenly tried to break his hold on her. "How—how can you say that when Luther's lying up there in that hospital in critical condition?"

Linc grabbed her hands tightly, forcing her into instant stillness. "Because it's true," he countered, his voice low and steady. "If anyone's been wronged in our coming together, it's been Jim—not your father. You've got to stop letting Luther rule your life. It's imperative that you cut the apron strings! Now."

She began weeping again. Deep soul-wrenching sobs shook her. It tore his heart to pieces, but he had to make her understand, to remove the guilt from her frail shoulders. He was fighting now, this moment, for his life, his future. It was too late to turn back. He was as committed to loving this woman as he was to breathing.

The first chance he got, he intended to make sure none of his team members ever opened their mouths in a derogatory manner about Keeley ever again. How in the hell had they found out he was seeing her in the first place? he wondered. It wouldn't do for him to come in contact with the ones responsible right now. The violence that clawed at his guts was so intense that he was afraid he'd be tempted to take a slice of their faces off with his fists. No wonder the old man had suffered a heart attack. Hearing his daughter's name slurred like that would be enough to raise anyone's blood pressure up and over the boiling point.

Suddenly he moved as if to stand up. Keeley clutched the front of his shirt in mindless panic.

"No, please, don't go. Hold me," she whispered, rivaling the sobs that choked her throat. She couldn't bear the thought of Linc leaving her. Regardless of her guilt or innocence concerning her father, she ached for Linc, for the security he offered. She was tired. She was hurt. She was frightened. The only thing that made any sense to her this minute was Linc. And his arms.

"Oh, baby, baby," he muttered, "you can rest assured I'm not going anywhere. At least not without you," he added, a ghost of a smile relieving the bleakness of his expression.

She nodded her head, her throat too full to speak.

"What you need right now more than anything else is rest," Linc said softly. Not giving her a chance to answer one way or the other, he calmly leaned over and scooped her light body up in his arms and headed in the direction of the bedroom.

He handled her as if he were afraid she would break. Every move he made was carried out with tenderness and loving care.

She let Linc help her remove her robe before once again crawling between the sheets. She then turned over on her side and rolled herself into a tight little ball.

Linc sat down on the bed beside her and watched, hoping to see her eyelids soon flutter shut. "Go to sleep, my love," he crooned.

Unable to remain still for long, she uncurled herself and turned trusting eyes in Linc's direction to make sure he was still beside her. Needing no further encouragement, he lay down next to her and took her into his arms. She let him hold her, wanting no more than to have him close.

Soon he eased his large frame into a more comfortable position, shifting Keeley's slight frame with him. Keeley wrapped her arms tighter around him and burrowed deeper, seeking his warmth. In that moment she felt she had learned the true meaning of love.

Love? She loved Linc. Oh, God! How could something so obviously wrong be so wonderfully right?

The battle that waged so furiously within her communicated itself to Linc. Mistaking her restlessness for deepening concern over her father, he began smoothing the hair away from her temple, leaving it open to the gentle touch of his lips.

"Don't worry, my darling, I'll always be here to share your burden." A shudder ran down his frame. "Don't you think I'm hurting, too? For you. For Luther. I think the world of that crotchety old fellow. The entire team and front office sends their love and sympathy, as well as everyone around the N.F.L. The commissioner has called every day, or so I'm told."

Keeley sighed against the solid wall of his chest. "I'll—I'll have to make a point to thank them all for their thoughts and kindness."

"Don't worry about it. Everyone knows you're grateful," he mouthed against her soft cheek as his hands again tried to coax her tensed-up limbs into complete relaxation.

At first the healing smoothness of his hands brought her the peace and consolation she sought, but without either of them consciously striving to alter the embrace, the quality of it began to change.

His hands now began to shuttle up and down her sleek back with tortured purpose. With care, he kissed the corners of her mouth, then eagerly sought the fullness of her lips. Their tongues met, increasing the furiosity of their clinging mouths.

Simultaneously, they both realized what was happening and froze. Pulling apart, they stared at each other in the muted glow of the subdued lamplight that

permeated the room. They were uncomfortably reminded of Luther and how ill he was.

Keeley felt a jolt of pain skid through her, almost
as if his touch had reached an exposed nerve. But was
it so terribly wrong to seek comfort and assuage the
sorrow she felt in the arms of the man she loved? Of
course it wasn't, she told herself. The time for apologies was over. She couldn't deny herself the right to
reach out and grab the chance to love for the first
time in her life. Linc had awakened her to its true and
glorious meaning. A sharing of this love now was not
an act of disrespect for her father; it was a release
from her past and a commitment to a new beginning.

"Linc—" An invitation sweetened his name.

"Oh, Keeley, lovely Keeley, you taste so good, so
sweet," he mumbled, looking deeply into her eyes.
"I want you so much, so much—"

"I know, I know," she breathed.

"But I'd hate myself for the rest of my life if I
took advantage of you now, especially with you being
so vulnerable, so—"

She placed warm lips against his mouth, forcing
him to swallow his unspoken words. "Please, I need
you," she whispered, her sweet breath caressing his
lips.

Nine

"And I need you," Linc choked against the satin softness of her neck while his hands were busy steadily lowering the straps of her gown from her shoulders.

An unconscious movement on her part made it possible for Linc to go ahead and completely remove the feather-light garment and fling it to the carpet.

He felt his throat constrict as she lay before him in ethereal beauty, the moonlight casting a golden sheen on her body. She was more perfect than he remembered, even though he thought he'd seared into his brain every perfect inch of her.

Suddenly feeling desperate to have nothing between them, he rolled over and off the bed in one swift move.

Unabashedly Keeley watched as he quickly removed each article of clothing in silence. Then he lowered himself beside her on the bed and stretched his full length against her.

After gently stroking her face with his hands, his mouth met hers. Linc worshiped it for long precious moments before moving lower to her breasts with the same thorough precision.

"I adore you," he murmured between nips. "You taste so good, so much like honey."

"Oh, yes, oh, wonderful." Her words were inarticulate cries; she had no control over her tongue as the sweet rapture continued.

Then his mouth seemed to be everywhere at once, using his moist kisses to bathe her limbs. He felt her silky and pliant flesh swell and come alive beneath the palm of his hand.

Keeley clutched at his hair and then his shoulders as arrows of desire penetrated her nervous system, piercing through her body.

He held her tight and let the flow of her passion run its true course.

Moments later, as she lay nestled in the crook of his arm, she began caressing his neck and shoulders with her tongue. She felt his straight, lean body tense beside her, followed by a shiver of anticipation. Her hands sought the treasures of his body with the same boldness with which he had sought hers.

"God, yes, Keeley, yes. Touch me!" he groaned in sweet agony.

Keeley looked at him. "Your skin is so soft, so smooth." There was a warm sweetness in her voice. "For an 'ole toughie' you have a beautiful body."

He groaned and quickly shifted their bodies so that he could look up into her eyes and drown himself in their illuminating and passionate glow. Then he reached up and placed his hand at the nape of her neck and lowered her head to meet his seeking lips.

As he reverently kissed her, he savored the delicious taste on her tongue. They explored together the hollowness of each other's mouth, making sure they had missed nothing from the last time they were together.

As her hands touched the deep shadows which

clung to the hollows of his strong face, Keeley felt his stirring hardness against her sensitive skin.

"Keeley," he gasped, "please—please—now!"

Suddenly Linc felt a tingle surge through his body from head to foot as she took him at his word and eased her small frame to mold with his, bringing them together gently, not thrusting or pushing, but descending in stages like the call of a whippoorwill, slow and beautiful.

As a joy as old as mankind flowed through Keeley's body, she felt she would surely die from the wonder of it.

Linc, in that same moment, felt he had just begun to live.

The lazy morning sunlight along with a feather-light tickling sensation against her cheek convinced Keeley to lift one eyelid. That was enough.

Linc's face, with a drawling grin splayed across it, filled her entire vision.

"I can say one thing for you, lovely Keeley, you do enjoy your sleep."

She straightened her legs and gave the covers a kick and then lifted her hands above her head and stretched every muscle in her body like a contented cat.

"If I had my way," she admitted, an impish smile covering her face, "I wouldn't be awake right now. But you just couldn't stand being awake alone, could you?"

"That's right, love," he teased. "Beautiful mornings aren't made for sleeping."

Before she could think of a choice rejoinder, a leering grin suddenly appeared on his face and he tossed

the covers to the foot of the bed and encased her in
a bone-crushing bear hug.

"Linc," she squeaked against his hard chest, but
her plea for mercy was lost as she came up with nothing but a mouthful of wiry hair in her bid for freedom
from his tight hold.

"I'll get even with you for this, Linc Hunter, if it's
the last thing I do," she hissed at him, although a
playful gleam teased her eyes.

"Baby, I surrender! Torture me any way you
please."

"You're crazy, did you know that?" she laughed
as she propped her elbows up on his chest and then
braced her chin in her hands.

"Crazy about you," he countered, his voice now
deep and serious, all trace of the lightheartedness
gone.

Keeley stared down into his eyes, and caught her
breath as his eyes spoke to her in gentle yearning.

There were no words to convey the intensity of her
feelings at this exact moment. Every bone and muscle
in her body had turned to pure liquid as she cradled
Linc's face in her hands and slowly lowered her lips
to his.

This touch ignited a flame within their hearts as
well as their bodies, and they gave themselves to each
other, this time in complete and wild abandonment.

"I want you to promise me one thing before I go,"
Linc said, cupping her face in his hand and bringing
it up to his line of vision.

"What is it?" Keeley questioned hesitantly as her
green eyes took in every detail of his scrubbed appearance. Although he hadn't been able to change his

clothes, he had taken a shower and shaved with one of her razors. He looked and smelled delicious.

"Please say that you'll attend the game this Saturday night."

Her eyes darkened. "I—I don't know. It depends on how Luther's getting along."

He sighed. "Of course, that goes without saying, but if he's better, will you come?"

Still she hesitated, averting her eyes.

He scraped his hand over his damp hair in agitation. "Believe me, I know how you feel. And I know we have a lot to talk about, but please humor me and say you'll come. We play the Dallas Cowboys and that's a big game." His eyes pleaded with her. "I need you to be there."

When he looked at her that way, Keeley could deny him nothing. Loosening her tongue, she said, "All right. Consider it a promise—if Dad's better, that is."

His eyes had grown shadowed. "I understand," he replied.

"When—when will I talk to you again?" She was reluctant for him to leave her, although she knew he must. They had dallied for too long as it was. She had to dress and get to the hospital, and Linc had to get to the field house for practice.

"I'll call you tonight," he promised as he leaned down and kissed her sweetly on the lips. Before Keeley realized his intentions, he opened the front of her robe and lowered his head still further to kiss the puckering roundness of her nipples. Keeley's heart pounded with hammering force against her ribs.

"I love these beauties," he muttered in a guttural tone as his hand continued its gentle play. "Just think, they'll soon be mine," he added. "All mine. To touch, to feel, and to love for as long as I live."

When the door closed quietly behind him, Keeley slowly wilted against the pillow, her body quivering like a heavy flower on a weak stalk.

Then a giddy feeling of pure pleasure replaced the weakness, pumping adrenaline through her veins at a rapid rate of speed. She was in love! It was wonderful! It was uniquely different! The only thing that kept her from laughing out loud and shouting her joy clear to the rooftop was her father. His lingering illness was a sobering force that couldn't be dispelled even in the wake of her newfound happiness.

In the dark recesses of her mind there still lay a pocket of guilt. Even though she knew that Linc was correct in making her face the fact that she could no longer live her life by her father's standards, she nevertheless couldn't render herself blameless. The entire episode had been such a hellacious nightmare that it would be a long time before she could completely clear her conscience. But on the other hand, she must keep in mind that no matter how much she loved her father and wanted his approval, her first allegiance was to herself.

Under no circumstances would she give up Linc. Her love for him and the intense satisfaction she found in his arms went beyond her wildest imagination. She knew he loved her; she felt it in his touch, saw it in his eyes and heard it in his voice. The words themselves weren't necessary now, she told herself. They would come; it was only a matter of time.

And on the heels of that conclusion followed another one: She was positive that when the commitment was actually voiced, he would tell her, at the same time, that he would give up his football career. He knew how she felt about it. Anyway, didn't he love his horses and his ranch and long to live there permanently? Hadn't he said as much to her? Of course, he had. With the great outdoors as their backdrop, she and Linc would build a home and create beautiful children. To have all that with the man she loved...what could be more perfect? It would work out. It had to.

But she had to shift Linc and the memories of their night together to the back of her mind and proceed to the hospital. Quickly she showered and shampooed her hair. Just when she finished buttoning her shirt, the telephone rang.

She dashed across the room and lifted the receiver.

"Hello," she murmured.

"Keeley, this is Judith."

"Good morning. Are you on your way to the hospital?"

"I'm already there," Judith answered, sounding cheerful but tired.

"How's—how's Dad?" Keeley could barely push the words through her tight throat.

"I'm delighted to report that he's much, much better," Judith replied happily. "In fact he's so much better Dr. Willis is considering having him transferred to a private room if he'll agree to having a private duty nurse full time."

"Thank God," Keeley breathed as she raised her head upward in silent thanks.

"Yes, isn't it wonderful." Judith sniffed and tried to control her shaky voice.

Even though she couldn't see her aunt, Keeley knew beyond a shadow of a doubt that tears of joy were streaming down her cheeks. Reaching up, she felt the moisture on her own face.

"Where are you now?" Keeley asked after a moment of silence while they both fought for control.

"I'm downstairs in the cafeteria."

"Good. Stay put and I'll be there shortly and join you for a cup of coffee. My first class isn't until eleven."

Hurriedly, Keeley stepped into her serviceable working sandals, and then glanced in the mirror to give her curls a final pat. She grabbed her favorite cologne, and was spraying each side of her neck when the piercing sound of the phone halted her again.

With a groan, she slammed down the bottle, covered the distance once again and lifted the ringing nuisance. At this rate she'd never get to the hospital.

"Yes," she said without preamble.

"Keeley?"

She grabbed the bedside table to steady herself as Jim's sober but perplexed voice sent shock waves rushing through her. Dear, sweet Jim. Dear God, much to her shame he had fled her mind as she'd reached the heights of rapture over and over in Linc's arms. How she hated to hurt him.

"Keeley, how's Luther?" he asked again, this time with more insistence.

"He—he's much better," she stammered as she tried to reorient her thoughts.

His thankful sigh of relief echoed through the receiver. "I'm not surprised. Somehow I knew that old man was a fighter and wouldn't give up." There was a short pause. "Give him my best when you see him today."

Keeley lowered herself wearily onto the bed. She

fought to keep the tears out of her voice. "I'm sure he'll appreciate your concern," she said softly.

There was no way that she could confide to Jim that her father refused to see her or talk to her. The pain was still too raw. But that wasn't even important anymore. Luther was on the road to recovery, and that was all that counted. The time for forgiving would come later.

"Are you planning to go to the university today?" Jim was asking, making an effort to trap her wandering mind.

"Yes, I am. I have an important lecture scheduled for every day this week. It's imperative that I be there."

There was a moment of strained silence.

"Will you call me later and let me know about Luther?" he asked at length, his voice sounding vague, far off.

She sighed. "You know I will. But now I really need to get off the phone and get to the hospital. I promise I'll call you later." She spoke in a clear, concise tone, trying to keep the edge off her voice.

"Keeley, let's get married. Now."

His words crackling through the telephone line had the same effect as lightning hitting a tree. For a moment, she felt dazed, incapacitated, unable to think coherently. Then slowly the shattered fragments of her mind began to fuse back together and with it came an acute sense of repulsion. There was a time and place for everything. This was certainly not the time or the place to tell Jim that she couldn't marry him, that she was in love with Linc and planning to marry him instead.

"Keeley? Will you?"

"Jim, please, not now. I—I don't—can't talk about us now. I must go. I'll talk to you later. Goodbye." With shaking hands, Keeley placed the receiver back into its cradle, grabbed her purse and slammed out the door.

"I was about to give you up, my dear," Judith said as she looked down at her watch. "What kept you?"

Keeley's brows puckered. "Jim caught me just as I got ready to walk out the door."

"Oh, and was that bad?"

"Well, yes, as a matter of fact it was," Keeley admitted, sitting down next to Judith and picking up her cup of now lukewarm coffee. "He's pressing me to marry him," she added with a forlorn sigh in her voice.

"Well, are you going to?"

"What?"

"Don't play dumb with me, Keeley Sanders! You know what."

Keeley's face was tight and drawn. "No—no, I'm not."

"Oh, I see," Judith remarked, turning her head to gaze about her.

"But you don't really, do you?" Keeley asked, feeling defeat settle heavily on her shoulders.

Judith turned her eyes to rest on Keeley once more. They were filled with love and understanding. She reached out and patted Keeley's hand.

"Yes, I do see. I know what you're going through with Jim and Linc. And I want you to know I'm on your side whatever you choose to do." She sighed and removed her hand. "I can't say that I'm not a little sorry that you aren't going to marry your staid college professor." A brief smile crossed her lips. "I thought he was perfect for you in every way. But who am I to say? I only want you to be happy, and if your happiness lies with Linc Hunter, then so be it. You have my blessing."

"Oh, Aunt Judith," Keeley began, her eyes shimmering with unshed tears. "I love you."

"And I love you," Judith stated. "And while we're in another one of our weepy sessions, I want to apologize for my rudeness to Linc the other evening. It was totally uncalled for and I'm sorry."

"Don't worry about it, Aunt Judith. None of us was responsible for what was said that night. We were all too upset to think rationally."

Judith shuddered. "That's for sure."

"Have you had a chance to talk to—to Dad this morning?"

Judith's eyes softened. "Yes, and we talked about you—"

"And?" Keeley interrupted.

"It's going to take time, my dear. He'll come around, you just wait and see. You must be patient."

A deep sigh rippled through Keeley. "I'll try."

"And I want you to promise me something else, too," Judith said. "I want you to give me your word that you won't let guilt eat away at your insides. I don't think it was the fact that you were seeing Linc that upset your father so much as the way in which he found out about it." She paused and cleared her throat. "It's a rule of thumb that most men can't tolerate slurs against their womenfolk or anyone else they love, for that matter."

Keeley cocked her head to one side. "By the way,

how do things stand with you and Dad now?'' She held her breath.

Judith toyed with her empty cup a minute and then flashed Keeley a bright smile. "Well, I was going to wait and tell you later, but since you ask.'' Her eyes sparkled. "The first thing your father did when he was able to talk was to ask me to marry him.''

"Oh, Aunt Judith, that's great!'' Keeley exclaimed excitedly. "If we weren't in such a public place, I'd jump up and hug you. It's about time my father came to his senses.''

"I don't have to tell you how happy I am,'' she said, laughing delightfully. "Now all we have to do is get him well and get you two straightened out and we'll have it made.''

A sweet smile spread across Keeley's face. "I'll second that,'' she said. "But for the moment I can be content knowing Dad is better and that soon you'll really and truly be my mother.''

Judith's eyes suddenly misted with tears. They stared at each other, oblivious to everyone else in the noisy room.

"Oh, Keeley,'' she said, sniffling back a sob, "you couldn't have paid me a higher compliment. I shall hold those words close to my heart always.'' She lowered her head and dug in her purse for a Kleenex. When she raised her head, she had regained control of her emotions.

"Aunt Judith, it's almost ten forty-five. I have to go now. My first class begins at eleven.''

"Goodness, I must get back upstairs too. Dr. Willis promised me that I could sit with your father in the unit while his room is being prepared.''

Keeley stood up and walked around the table and

stood next to Judith. Leaning over, she gave her a peck on her delicately scented skin. "Give my love to Dad," she whispered before turning on her heel and making her way across the room and out the door into the beautiful crisp morning.

There was a springy bounce to her stride as she walked to the car. The whole world suddenly looked rosy! And why not? She had Linc. Her father was on the road to recovery and soon to be married. His forgiveness and understanding was surely imminent. She hoped that he would even welcome Linc into the family, *after* he got over the shock of losing his ace quarterback to his daughter and to a horse ranch. This last thought was added with a silent chuckle.

Her life was definitely full of new promise, and she aimed to make the most of it.

The cold night air welcomed Keeley as she made her way into the Superdome. She felt a shiver of anticipation race down her spine at the thought of seeing Linc again, even if it was from afar.

Although the past few days had been happy ones for her, there was a twinge of frustration mixed in with the happiness. She hadn't seen Linc. She had talked to him on the phone every day, but it wasn't the same. Hearing his voice certainly didn't take the place of having his strong arms around her.

They had both been busy during the week. She had stayed late at work to tutor one of her students and had kept a close check on her father. Linc had also been busy, training hard and getting ready for the big game between the Timberjacks and the Cowboys. Many had lauded the game as being a preview of Super Bowl XVII.

She yearned to talk to Linc about their future. There was so much that still needed to be said and so many plans to be made. But they could wait. She felt secure in his love and was for the most part perfectly content. The only flies in the ointment were Jim and her father. She hadn't yet found the words to tell Jim about Linc. Although her woman's intuition told her that he wouldn't be at all surprised or shocked, she nevertheless dreaded hurting him.

And of course, there was her father. He was improving every day. But to her sorrow, he remained adamant about refusing to see her. However, she was confident that he would soon relent and all would be resolved between father and daughter once more.

As she took her seat in her father's private box seat section, she couldn't help but feel the excitement in the air around her. For a moment, she longed to share this game with the flag-waving, foot-stomping crowd below her in the regular stands. They always seemed to enjoy every minute of the game to the fullest. But she was where she belonged.

A sound behind her caught her attention as she was making herself comfortable in her seat. Turning around, she saw Stan Engles, her father's partner, and his wife, Millie, coming toward her.

Keeley smiled. "Hello, Millie. How are you? Long time, no see," she said, making polite but meaningless conversation.

"Oh, I'm just great, and you?" Millie huffed as she lowered her slightly overweight body into the chair next to Keeley.

"I'm fine," Keeley answered, already becoming bored with the exchange of pleasantries. It wasn't that she had anything against Millie Engles. She just didn't want to be bothered with having to make idle conversation throughout the game. She wanted her mind and thoughts free to concentrate on Linc.

But she was denied this privilege, at least for a while, anyway. Next there was Stan to be reckoned with, followed by several other members of the Timberjack staff. Of course, she had to be polite and gracious. They were all concerned about her father, and more than anxious to do anything they could to help. By the time she spoke to each one and assured them of Luther's slow but sure recovery, the crowd was on their feet to welcome the Timberjacks onto the field.

From that moment on, Keeley was oblivious to everything and everyone around her. Everyone, that is, except number twelve. The appearance of Linc's big brawny body on the field instantly filled her vision as well as her heart. She felt it swell with love and pride. He looked so confident, so much in command, so dear. *And so vulnerable,* she thought with painful honesty. Suddenly, she felt her stomach lurch as goose bumps popped out on her skin. She was afraid. Sinking her teeth into her lower lip, she glanced around her.

The spectators were the key. Their emotions were high—too high. Keeley realized that, to them, this was no ordinary game. They hadn't attended this game merely to cheer their favorite team to victory. It was more than that, much more. It was apparent that the entire sea of bodies and faces on their feet yelling and screaming were out for blood, the Dallas Cowboys' blood.

She felt her own blood curdle again at the thought of Linc being a part of this fearsome and hard-hitting sport. She longed with renewed urgency to hear it from his lips that he would give it all up at the end of the season, for himself as well as for her. She prayed that he would get through this game unhurt.

At the end of the first quarter, she realized that her nagging worries had all been in vain. Linc performed brilliantly, as did his teammates. She was right about one thing though: It was a contest played in vengeance. Every time it looked as if Linc was going to be sacked, she closed her eyes and gritted her teeth. By the time the half rolled around, Keeley felt as if she, too, had played each down. Perspiration dampened her skin, and her fingers were numb from squeezing them together so tightly.

As the half-time activities were beginning, she stood up. Suddenly her muscles unlocked; she felt weak and limp as a ragdoll.

"Are you all right, Keeley?" Stan Engles asked, placing a tentative hand on her arm. "You look ill," he added bluntly.

Keeley turned toward him, forcing a smile to her lips. "I'm fine, Stan. I just felt weak for a moment." She looked around her and noticed with an embarrassed frown on her face that several others were peering at her with strange and curious expressions on their faces.

"Where's—where's Millie?" she stammered inanely, desperately wanting to draw the attention from herself.

Stan drew his handkerchief out of his back pocket and wiped his mouth before answering. "She's gone to the ladies' room. Left right before the half." He laughed. "She wanted to beat the crowd." He paused again and scrutinized her closely. "I'm surprised you didn't notice when she left. You certainly must have been out of it for a few minutes."

Keeley felt her face blush with color. "When I'm watching a game, I always tend to lose myself in it," she lied without so much as blinking an eye.

A light sprang into his eyes. "Now that's a woman after my own heart," he teased. "Luther's damn lucky to have a daughter like you who's not only got a capable head on her shoulders for business but also enjoys the sport as well. Now take my wife and daughter," he went on without even taking another breath, "they barely know a football from a basketball. Only reason Millie comes with me is out of duty."

Keeley smiled. "Thank you for those kind words, Stan," she said politely. "I'll be sure and pass them on to Dad." She paused and reached down to pick up her purse. Enough was enough, she thought. She couldn't take much more of Mr. Stan Engles, partner or no partner. But none of her seething discontent showed as she looked up at him. "If you'll excuse me now, I must follow your wife."

"Hurry back!" he called to her retreating back. "You don't want to miss a minute of this second half. We're going to send 'em back to Texas in shreds."

"Whew!" Keeley breathed aloud as she made her way out of the box and into the adjoining lounge. The warm peacefulness of the room was like a balm to her battered senses. If she'd thought about it, she would have parked herself at one of the tables by the plate glass windows and watched the game from there, minus all her father's cronies! It was a heavenly thought, but unfortunately it came too late. She was positive that if she didn't return to her seat in the

V.I.P. section, Stan or Millie would come looking for her.

Rushing to the ladies' room, she washed her clammy hands, ran a powder puff over her nose and gazed at herself critically in the ceiling-to-floor mirror.

Would Linc find the new outfit she'd chosen especially for this game attractive? She certainly hoped so. She had gone on a two-day crash spending spree and splurged on this three-piece suit of wool and rayon in a soft muted cranberry. The skirt was slit up both sides, just enough to give one an alluring vision of her smoothly shaped calves. An off-white silk blouse tied at the neck in a casual bow, complemented by the matching jacket, made her feel chic but at the same time all female with an aim to please her man.

Giving her soft shiny curls a pat, she smiled before making her way out the door. By the time she found herself seated beside Millie once again, the second half was under way.

Immediately the same feeling of panic clawed at her insides as Linc scrambled out of the pocket to try to find Jake Donovan, his favorite tight end to throw the football to. She sank her teeth into her lower lip and grasped the chair arms with all her strength as Linc finally released the ball. Jake leapt into the air with all the energy of a pole vault jumper, brought the ball down and clutched it to his chest. He ran like a streak of lightning toward the goal post.

"That's the way to fake 'em out of their breeches, Linc, my boy," Stan yelled. "Give 'em hell!"

"Shhh, Stan, not quite so loud," Millie ordered, throwing an apologetic look in Keeley's direction.

But Keeley couldn't have cared less who was yelling or how loud. Although not verbal herself, she was just as eager for Jake to score a touchdown as the next person. In fact, she had more at stake. If the Timberjacks lost this game, Linc would be devastated. It was "a matter of pride," or so he had explained to her one night over the phone. "They beat us like we were yard dogs last year," he'd said, "and we're looking to turn the tables come Saturday night."

She couldn't help but shudder as she thought about that conversation. With the score tied seven all, she knew how concerned Linc must be feeling at this very minute. With the third quarter nearing an end, it was quickly turning into a defensive game, which could mean only one thing: open warfare. No quarterback wanted the defense to have to carry more than its share of the load.

The sounds of disgust riveting through the ninety-thousand-plus fans put a stop to her wandering thoughts. The referee's whistle was blowing loud and clear, indicating the fourth and final down. The Timberjacks had to give up the football. It was a dejected offensive team that left the field.

Keeley was worried. She sincerely hoped that Judith was managing to keep her father away from the television set. This type of suspense wasn't good for a healthy person's heart, she thought, much less one who was unhealthy.

"Defense! Defense! Defense!" The fans were shouting, their voices loud and boisterous. It seemed as if everyone in the stadium was chanting, including herself.

"Do you think we're going to win, Keeley?" Millie asked, her voice irritatingly loud and squeaky.

Keeley swallowed her vexation. "I hope so," she answered, hurriedly turning her attention back to the game. She certainly didn't want to appear rude to Millie Engles, but on the other hand, she didn't want to encourage any small talk between them either.

For the remainder of the third quarter and a few minutes into the fourth one, Keeley watched as the game seesawed back and forth with neither team gaining any ground.

Each time Linc got his hands on the football, she felt fear rise within her. The front line of the Dallas Cowboys, led by big Harvey Martin and Ed "Too Tall" Jones, was determined to keep Linc from completing any passes.

But Linc was determined. The Timberjacks were on the twenty-yard line, deep into Cowboy territory. The count was second down and eight yards to go for another Timberjack first down.

Keeley felt her heart slam forward in her chest as Linc stepped out of the pocket and reared back to throw.

Then it happened. Just as Linc released the ball and sent it sailing through the air directly into the arms of a wide receiver, Harvey Martin came at him from the side and buried his helmet into Linc's body with bone-crushing force.

Keeley watched in horrified silence as Linc's head snapped backward. Then, as if in slow motion, she saw his whole body lunge forward and fall into a crumpled heap onto the hard turf.

"Are you Keeley Saunders?"

Keeley whirled around to confront the calm and attractive nurse who had come unobtrusively into the waiting room. Keeley's eyes were wide with terror as she waited for the woman to speak.

Keeley saw a look of sympathy soften her expression before she spoke in a soft voice. ''Mr. Hunter is now in a private room on the third floor, and he's asking for you.''

Relief made Keeley ill. She felt a wave of nausea wash over her. She closed her eyes and groped frantically for the wall to help maintain her balance.

''Please, lean on me and take deep breaths,'' the nurse demanded as her warm hands gently circled Keeley's waist and helped her into the nearest chair. ''Now, you sit still while I get a damp cloth and sponge your face.'' She paused momentarily and smiled down at Keeley. ''Don't worry, your friend is going to be all right.''

Keeley forced herself to do as the nurse told her, though she wanted to tear out of the room and upstairs to Linc.

But her body was her own worst enemy. She was too weak to move, and still too nauseated. She rested her head back against the chair and breathed deeply through her mouth. God, how she hated having the weak trembles.

She guessed that she was lucky to have gone this long before her mental despair rendered her body useless. She remembered seeing Linc's limp body, unmoving, lying on the field, though her actions from that moment on were still blurred in her mind.

She remembered swallowing a cry of pain before latching onto her purse and jacket and tearing out of the reserved section as though mad demons were in pursuit of her. Somehow she managed to make it to the hospital, where she was positive she would find Linc's mangled and torn-up body already in surgery.

She also remembered the hushed silence that had descended over the crowd as they waited for the stretcher to remove Linc's inert body. She could still hear the echo of Stan Engles's words as she had made her panicky flight out the door. "What the hell's the matter with her? Where's she going in such an all-fired hurry?"

The wait had been long and hard. By the time she ran through the swinging doors of the hospital, Linc was already in the emergency room. Two of the Timberjack trainers were closeted with him. She had been kept in the dark as to his condition until the nurse had sought her.

As the nurse bathed Keeley's face with adept, soothing motions, Keeley felt the shaky feeling disappear from her limbs.

"Thank you so much, nurse," she said, a grateful smile crossing her white lips. "If you'll tell me the room number, I'll be on my way. And thank you again for your help."

"You're more than welcome. Glad I could help."

With number three-thirteen imbedded on her brain, Keeley rode the elevator to the third floor. Stepping off, she dashed into the nearest ladies' room and hastily repaired her ravaged features. She hated to face Linc with dried tears on her cheeks.

She knocked lightly on the door and then waited a few seconds before pushing the heavy door slowly back and peering into the dimly lighted room.

Keeley felt her heart turn over in her breast as she tiptoed further inside the room and came to stand beside the bed. She stared down at the still, pale face

of the man she loved. *Oh, dear Lord, I can't stand
any more of this. I love him too much!*

She moved to clasp his limp fingers into hers. Her
sudden motion brought Linc's eyes open with a start.
Recognizing Keeley, a relieved smile twisted the corners of his mouth.

"Before you say anything," he whispered, "I'm
all right. And I love you."

"Oh, Linc," she mouthed, her throat too swollen
to speak. The tears were again flowing down her
cheeks.

"Shhh, dry up those tears and roll this cantanker-
ous bed up so I can talk to you. I was never one for
lying flat on my back."

Keeley quickly pressed the button labeled "head."

"Now before anything else, I want to hold you.
But be careful, my love," he cautioned, smiling
wanly. "My ribs are taped up tighter than Dick's hat-
band."

Her throat still too dry with fear and emotion to
say anything, Keeley leaned over and laid her head
in the crook of his arm, being careful not to put any
pressure on his sore chest.

"How—how seriously are you hurt?" she finally
stammered, the hot tears scalding both their faces as
she nestled closer to him, as though she were a
wounded animal.

"I have a concussion and several broken ribs." He
paused and laid his lips gently against her temple. "If
I behave myself, I'll be able to get out of here by
tomorrow or the next day."

"Thank God," she stressed as she lifted her head
so that she could look Linc in the eyes. "I—I died a
thousand deaths while I waited to hear how seriously

hurt you were.'' She traced a finger around his eyes and then down his cheek to his lips.

"I knew you would be worried," he said, capturing her hand and turning her palm upward to rest against his mouth. His breath fanned that sensitive part of her skin as he continued, "I sent word to find you the minute I regained consciousness."

"Are you sure you just have a slight concussion?"

"I'm sure," he murmured absently, obviously tired of talking about himself.

But Keeley wasn't convinced. She was still deeply concerned about his injuries. It was easy for him to slough them off as nothing, but she couldn't. If only this football season were already over, she thought with a growing despondency. How could she stand another two months of constantly worrying about him? Her mind was in a turmoil.

Slowly she stood up and walked across the room to gaze out the window, her back to Linc.

"Keeley, if I scoot over on the bed, will you come and lie down beside me?" His voice was soft and spine-tingling and sensuous. "I want to hold you. I want to feel your soft breasts rub up against me. I want to taste your lips. I—" He paused abruptly and Keeley stood still, too disoriented by the seduction of his words to move.

Suddenly, she felt hands on her upper arms and was being slowly turned around.

She stared up into Linc's pale but determined face. "Since you wouldn't come to me, I came to you," he said softly.

"Oh, Linc," Keeley cried, "you shouldn't have gotten out of bed. Your—your ribs! You'll hurt them! Please, let—"

"You talk too damn much, my love," he scolded as he drew her tenderly against his scantily clad body. "Anyway," he added, teasing the graceful slant of her neck, "they've got my ribs taped so damned tight I can't feel a thing! So stop worrying. We have more important things to take care of at the moment."

There was no need for his reprimand. The instant Keeley's arms circled him and her hands came into contact with his bare skin of his upper buttocks, she was lost.

She heard Linc's deep moan as his mouth swooped down and claimed hers in a soul-searing kiss. They clung together until there was no air left in their lungs. Only then did Linc release her.

"Oh, Keeley, I can't wait until we're married," he rasped. "There are so many ways I want to love you." His hands were moving up and down her spine in loving devotion.

"I know, I feel the same way," she whispered urgently. "And I can't wait for the season to be over, so we can leave the city. Then you'll never have to pick up a football again."

Suddenly a strangled sound erupted from Linc's lips, and his hands ceased all movement.

For a moment, Keeley thought he was in pain, but when he slowly pushed her out of his arms and she saw the marble coldness in his eyes, she knew it wasn't pain but anger that caused the abrupt change.

A puzzled frown marred her delicate features as she stared up at him. "Linc?"

"Where did you get the idea that when we married I was going to give up football?"

The silence that descended over the tiny sterile

room was ominous, with the potential to erupt like a spewing volcano.

Keeley's heart hung suspended between her stomach and her toes. "I—I just assumed you would, knowing how I—I feel about it." Her voice had dwindled to nothing.

A strange light appeared in the narrow hardness of his eyes. "I'm sorry if you got that impression," he said coldly, "but nothing could be further from the truth." He turned away, his back straight, and plodded with measured precision back to the bed.

Keeley felt as if she had been stabbed in the heart! Her first thought was to scream, *No, you can't do this to me!* But she said nothing. She stood like a zombie and forced herself to swallow the burning heat that threatened to strangle her.

"Keeley," Linc said quietly, breaking into the smothering silence, "I'm not like Paul."

"I know you're not," she answered through tight, stiff lips, her back ramrod straight as she turned and stared at him.

"Then it shouldn't bother you that I play football for a living. I'm not interested in women or partying. I'm only interested in loving you—for as long as I live."

Keeley felt tears prick her eyes. She blinked them back. "That's what I want too," she said in a strangled whisper, "but—"

"But what?" he interrupted, his expression tightening at her persistent stubbornness.

"I—I swore I'd never live that kind of life again." Unchecked tears slid down her pale cheeks. "I can't stand the uncertainties such as never knowing if you'll come out of a game without getting seriously hurt—like now for instance.''

"Keeley, please listen to me. You're—"

"No, Linc! You listen to me. I want a husband who can offer me security, stability and a loving home life." Her voice broke and for a moment she couldn't go on. Then her voice regained a thread of its former strength. "I can't settle for less."

"And I can't be or make myself into something I'm not," he countered quietly. "You must take me as I am or—" His voice halted as if he too was having trouble speaking.

Another profound silence shook the room as they stared at each other with both their hearts twisting in pain.

"Or what?" Keeley finally whispered, stifling a hurt that went far beyond words and tears.

"Or not at all."

"Is that your final word?"

"No, damn it, it's not," he exclaimed harshly. "If my love isn't enough, then so be it. You just go ahead and take the easy way out. Go marry your no-nonsense professor. If being safe and living in a vacuum means more to you than everything else, then who am I to argue?"

On legs that felt as if they were imbedded in concrete, she took a tentative step toward him. "Linc, please try to understand—"

Linc drew in a deep, harsh breath. "There's nothing to understand, Keeley," he said tautly. "It's obvious that our definition of love isn't the same." He turned his back toward her. "If you don't mind, please close the door behind you."

If Linc had plunged a knife straight through her

heart, she couldn't have been in more pain. Numb with grief, she somehow found her way to the door, the tears stinging her cheeks in blinding force. She paused for a breathless second.

Then without a backward glance, Keeley pushed the door open and walked through it. She was conscious of nothing except the sobs that shook her slender body with brutish force.

Ten

"I'm pregnant, Aunt Judith."

"You didn't have to tell me that, my dear," Judith countered softly. "You've been flashing signs of a woman with child for the last two months."

Keeley couldn't hold back a laugh at her aunt's old-fashioned way of describing pregnancy. But just as quickly as the smile appeared it vanished from her soft lips, leaving them curved downward in a despondent grimace.

"Exactly how far along are you?" Judith asked, a concerned pucker now distorting her forehead.

"About two and a half months." Keeley smiled weakly. "I saw a doctor today and that's about as close as he and I could get."

Judith released her breath slowly. "Have you told Linc?"

"No!" Keeley announced strongly, then tempered her tone somewhat before continuing. "And I'm not going to, either." Her softer, but still defiant, tone dared Judith to argue with her.

"Keeley," Judith began.

"Please, Aunt Judith," Keeley interrupted. "I—I don't, can't talk about Li—Linc right now."

"I'm sorry. I didn't mean to upset you," Judith

apologized, her eyes pools of loving sympathy. "When you're ready to talk, I'll listen."

Keeley nodded wordlessly as she settled herself more comfortably on the couch. Even the mention of Linc's name had the power to tear her to pieces these days.

"What are your plans, then?" Judith asked following a moment of silence.

Keeley sighed. "Now that the term's over here at the university, I'm going to resign and move home, to Eugene. I can have my old position back at U. of O."

"Oh, Keeley," Judith cried, "I hate to see you leave. Alone—pregnant! Won't you reconsider and stay where we can take care of you?"

"I can't, Aunt Judith. I—I can't stay in Portland any longer—especially now." Her last words came out in a choked whisper.

"Don't go upsetting yourself again," Judith cautioned hurriedly. "I only want what will make you happy. Don't mind me. I'm just a sentimental old fool who's being selfish."

Keeley smiled. "You're anything but that. And I hate to hurt you or seem ungrateful to you and Dad, but..."

"Consider the matter closed. I'll stand behind you no matter what you choose to do."

There was another moment of silence as Judith left her chair and stepped into her cheerful kitchen where she poured herself another cup of coffee and Keeley a glass of fruit juice.

When Judith handed Keeley the chilled beverage, she asked, "What about Jim?"

Keeley's eyes flew up to Judith's face. "I haven't told him," she said dejectedly.

"He's a good man. He'll understand."

"There's nothing for him to understand. There's no way I can marry him now, Aunt Judith. Not while another man's child is living inside of me. Surely you couldn't think otherwise?" Keeley added, her eyes wide and incredulous.

Judith couldn't quite meet her eyes. "Well—it was just a thought." She colored. "But only if Jim knew the score right from the start."

"Oh, Aunt Judith!" Keeley cried, tears filling her eyes.

"I know how that must sound to you," Judith defended herself, "but I was thinking of what's best for you, the baby, and your—your father."

Keeley felt goose bumps crawl over her body. "I'm—I'm not ready to tell Dad yet." She paused and moistened her dry lips. "I'm afraid—until his heart becomes stronger, that is."

Judith seemed to grow weak with relief. "I think that's a wise decision for now," she conceded. "When the time is right to tell him, you'll know. And everything will be fine. Just fine."

"I hope you're right."

"I know I'm right. You just wait and see," Judith said with firm conviction as she sat down beside Keeley and placed an arm around her shoulders.

Silently they embraced one another for a long moment. When they parted, Keeley felt better.

"I—I guess I'll go home now," Keeley said as she stood up and made her way toward the door, "and let you get some rest. I know you must be exhausted." She smiled. "You need to be as fresh as a daisy for the wedding tomorrow night."

"Pooh," Judith returned, "you're the one that needs the rest." She grinned. "I'm in perfect shape and ready to go."

"Just think, Aunt Judith, in less than twenty-four hours, you'll be Mrs. Luther Cooper."

"And I can't wait," Judith exclaimed excitedly, then gave Keeley one final hug before closing the door behind her.

The minute Keeley let herself into her apartment, she kicked off her shoes and walked into the bedroom. Not bothering to remove her dress or even her pantyhose, she fell across the bed in an exhausted heap. The tears were a cleansing blessing as they flooded her eyes and then drenched her face.

How on earth could I, a supposedly educated and smart woman, get myself into such a disastrous mess? Three months pregnant! But why, all of a sudden, was she acting so surprised? Any time a woman slept with a man and took no precautions, then she had to be prepared to face the music and pay the piper if and when the day of reckoning came.

Well, payday had finally come. And she was paying in double doses.

She'd had a good idea that she was pregnant even before she went to the doctor, but she hadn't been prepared to face it. And she still wasn't. "Oh, Linc! Linc!" she sobbed miserably as she turned over and pounded the pillow with her fists.

Since the day he had practically thrown her out of his hospital room, her thoughts had centered around Linc and the pain and confusion of their parting. November and December had slipped by practically unnoticed as she made herself get up every morning and go to the university. For those few hours a day, she joined the world of the living; it was impossible not to. The students were a lively group and demanded not only her undivided attention but an alert brain as well. She had to work hard to stay one step ahead of them.

Even Christmas failed to perk her up. The whole holiday season passed in a blur, as did all the other days. There was nothing that could fill the void that losing Linc had created. It was as if she had left part of herself in the hospital that fateful day, and she couldn't seem to get herself back on track without the missing part.

Never had her mind known such agony. She fought the same battle daily. She should have known better than to trust him. *Love* these days certainly wasn't synonymous with devotion and self-sacrifice, she kept reminding herself. Linc didn't love her. She was positive he'd *never* loved her. Football was all he needed to make his life complete. Their brief time together was over! Finished! She had to remember that in order to survive.

The only salvageable thing to come out of her days during this dark period was that she had made peace with her father. With determination and the love of Judith spurring him on, he had improved slowly but surely. Without a doubt, Judith was also Keeley's champion, and responsible for healing the festering wound that lay open between them.

Luther was a changed man. Since he had found out that he wasn't going to die and that he hadn't lost Judith, his life had new meaning. Even though his illness had taken a further toll on his body, his mind was still quick as ever, and he was softer, less rigid and stubborn.

Keeley remembered the day she had slipped into his room while the nurse had gone for coffee. She had been determined to see him with or without his permission. Although his eyes had been closed, she had known he wasn't asleep....

"Who's there?" he asked, slowly turning over on his back.

"It's me, Dad."

Luther's eyes narrowed in his gaunt face, and for a moment Keeley was afraid he was going to demand that she leave.

She held her breath and blinked back the tears as she took in his appearance. This attack, she knew, had just about left her an orphan. Each time he suffered one, it left him a little weaker, making him older and more frail. The grayish tint of his skin and shocking amount of weight that seemed to have vanished from his bones brought home to Keeley once again just how lucky she was to still have him alive.

"What are you staring at, girl?" he asked brusquely. His gruffly spoken words severed her rumbling thoughts.

"You, Dad. I'm staring at you," she said softly as she smiled through her tears.

"Dry up those tears now, girl, do you hear me?" he demanded weakly.

Did his voice catch on a sob? Keeley wondered as she moved her chair closer to the bed.

"I'm alive," he said. "Now's a time for celebration, not tears.'' Then he smiled and raised a trembling hand, bringing it to rest against her wet cheek.

"Oh, Dad," she cried, turning her face into the limp palm. "I'm so sorry, so sorry," she added, her voice an agonizing whisper.

"Not nearly as sorry as I am."

His confession caught Keeley off guard. Had she heard him right? Had he actually apologized to her?

She turned her head away from his hand and stared at him. Using the hand that she had dropped, he motioned for her to come even closer. She bent over him and waited.

"You heard me right." His dull-toned eyes were filled with tears. "Without my two girls, life wouldn't be worth living, anyway. I must remember that I can't mold your life to suit me—" He paused, obviously searching for the strength to continue. "That it's your life and you must live it as you see fit."

"Oh, Daddy, I love you," Keeley sobbed, burying her head into the crook of his arm, letting the tears flow in force.

When there were no more tears left to cry, Keeley raised her head. "About Linc—and me, Dad. It's—it's over."

"Shhh, it doesn't matter," he said patting her bowed head. "I want no explanations. If Linc is what you want and he can make you happy, then that's what I want too." A weak smile filtered through his voice. "I'll even gracefully give up my star quarterback if that's what it takes to make my girl happy."

Keeley gulped back another sob and shook her head sadly. "It's—it's too late. It's all over. But don't think for one minute it was your fault," she declared emphatically, "because it wasn't. You had nothing to do with it."

He seemed to accept her words as the truth and in doing so made it possible for them to mend the bridge of lost communication and misunderstanding that had separated them for so long. Her visits increased in length and frequency both at the hospital and then at home, creating a closeness between father and daughter that they had never before shared.

Being welcome in her own home once again had helped ease the cold, deep void of emptiness that she carried inside her. Somehow she had even mercifully managed to keep thoughts of Linc from dominating her every waking hour of every day....

Until today.

When every last tear was squeezed from her heart, Keeley rolled over on to her back and unconsciously placed a hand on her stomach. *She and Linc, together, had made a baby!* Even with the doctor's confirmation still ringing in her ears, she was finding it hard to believe.

As soon as she'd left the doctor's office she'd gone straight to Judith's. This was the first time she had been alone to really think about the marvel that was taking place within the complicated framework of her body.

Instead of the pain and misery that she should have been feeling, she suddenly felt fiercely protective of the tiny life that soon would be hers, and hers alone, to rear and to make into the finest human being she possibly could. The challenge was waiting to be met.

No more tears from you, Keeley Sanders! No more wallowing in self-pity! She had picked up the shattered pieces of her life once before. She could do it again. After all, she had a lot to be thankful for: her family, her health, her job. *But most of all she had the miracle growing within her.* She could rebuild her future and be content. Couldn't she?

The lights from her father's house shone with twinkling brightness as Jim parked his Cutlass in back of the house.

Turning toward Keeley, he smiled, "I can't believe your father and Judith are finally tying the knot after all these years. Luther's getting himself one fine woman."

Keeley smiled in return. "I couldn't agree with you more. I've been looking forward to this day all of my life," she said gently, a rapt expression on her face.

Laughter and strains of beautiful music greeted them as Keeley pushed open the rear door of the house. The smell of flowers, richly perfuming the air, was another indication of the party-like atmosphere.

She took one step into the room and then suddenly came to a frozen stop. She quickly sucked in a deep breath and closed her eyes, hoping to ward off the dizziness that threatened to overwhelm her. After what seemed like forever, but in reality was only seconds, Keeley opened her eyes, positive that she was hallucinating. But the man in the rear of the crowded living room was no hallucination. It was Linc Hunter in the flesh. All one hundred and ninety pounds of him leaning negligently against the doorframe.

In Keeley's subconscious mind flashed the thought that this was an instant replay of the first time she had seen him. But that wasn't possible. Nothing ever stayed the same. So many things had changed. It seemed as if she had lived a lifetime since she'd met Linc.

Then she panicked. The blood in her veins turned to ice water as she instinctively placed one hand across her stomach while digging deeper into the rail with the other one.

What was he doing here? Would he guess her secret? He knew her so intimately, not only her body but her mind as well. Was the change in her body obvious? She could not let him know—

"Keeley, are you all right?" Jim cried as he moved toward her. He arrived just in the nick of time to catch her limp form in his arms.

Her eyelids fluttered open slowly. She realized that she was lying in her bedroom, the glow of a lamp creating a shadow on the wall.

"How do you feel, honey?" Judith's voice crooned softly. "You gave us all such a fright."

Sitting beside the bed, Judith lifted Keeley's hand and cradled it within her own.

Keeley turned on her side and looked at Judith with tears pouring from her eyes. "I'm—I'm so sorry," she whispered.

"There's nothing to be sorry for." She smiled. "It's not unusual for pregnant women to faint, you know."

Keeley frowned as she blinked back the tears. "Linc. I saw Linc, Aunt Judith." She barely managed to get the words out of her mout:.

Judith shook her head. "No. You're mistaken. You couldn't have seen Linc. Your father didn't invite him."

"I saw Linc," Keeley repeated dully, listlessly.

Judith frowned deeply. "Will you be all right for a moment? I want to go speak to your father and let Jim know you're all right." She leaned over and kissed Keeley on the forehead. "I'll be back shortly."

The minute Judith left the room, Keeley sat up on the side of the bed and then on wobbly legs crossed the room to stand by the window. She leaned her head against the windowsill and stared out into the star-glazed darkness.

Linc. The father of her unborn child.

Would he continue to haunt her for the rest of her life no matter what she did? Because of him, she had done the one thing that she swore she wouldn't do. She had thrown a kink into the wedding ceremony.

But seeing Linc again after weeks of heart-wrenching loneliness and misery was more than her body and her mind could take. She had crumbled from within. As tears dripped from her eyes and ran down her face she wondered if she would ever be able to put herself back together again.

"Keeley?"

Her breath froze in her chest. She held her body in bondage for a moment—programming it not to move or to speak.

"Keeley...are you—you all right?" Linc asked, his voice soft and agonizingly dear.

She felt her body come alive and slowly turn around. At first, the combination of the dim lighting in the room and her eyes, flooded with tears, blinded her. Rapidly she blinked her eyes until the tiny drop-lets of pain no longer hampered her vision. Her gaze fastened upon Linc's intent face.

He was just as strong and beautiful as ever. He looked impeccable in a charcoal gray suit tailored to fit his large frame, trimming his overabundant thigh muscles to perfection.

His eyes were as clear and piercing as ever. And his mouth was the same thin but exquisitely tender one that had branded her skin over and over again with ardent delight. Taking a step forward and then halting, she noticed the grooves had deepened considerably around his lips. She hadn't remembered them being there.

"Hello, Linc," she said inanely, stifling the quake that threatened to erupt in her voice.

Keeley's greeting was met with silence as Linc's eyes seemed to penetrate through to her very soul. She fought like a caged wild bird to remove her eyes from his. But she couldn't. She was trapped by his steadfast gaze.

Sweet Jesus, but she's breathtaking! Linc thought as he stood overwhelmed at the sight of her. The thin beam of light that fell over the room seemed to praise her beauty. Her reddish blond curls clung to her head like a shining halo—a perfect foil for the unpretentious silk dress that clung to her body in provocative detail.

And her breasts, he thought, were perfection personified as they pushed and pouted with urgency against the soft material. He wanted to sweep her up into his arms and nestle his head between those shields of her womanhood in prelude to slowly undressing her and tasting the sweetness of her supple skin. How he longed to be inside of her, to feel himself expand within her.

Yet he couldn't move. He couldn't tell her how he felt. Why? Because he couldn't stand the thought of her telling him to leave her alone, to stay out of her life. He couldn't bear to hear a repeat of all the vile things he said to her the last time they were together.

He would never forgive himself; how could he expect her, the recipient of his verbal abuse, to do so?

He was a damned loser. The sooner he faced it, the better off he would be. He had to get out of her life before he brought her any more pain and heartache. Hadn't he wreaked enough havoc already to last her a lifetime?

God! How much he still loved her! But with this knowledge came the gut-wrenching fact that he had lost her.

The sight of her, an alluring smile covering her entire face, and the enticing swell of her body, more inviting and full than ever before, would have to last him during this lifetime and beyond.

For he was certain that he would never be welcome in her arms again.

The soft whisper of Keeley's indrawn breath forced Linc to cease his self-denunciation. A muscle jerked in his jaw as he forced himself to speak. "I didn't want to intrude." He paused as if he were at a loss for words. Then he went on. "But I had to make sure you were all right before I left."

Keeley's eyes refused to budge from his face. "I'm—I'm fine," she declared softly.

He frowned. "You really should see a doctor. This is twice now that you've fainted—" His voice trailed off on a soft and helpless note.

When Keeley didn't respond, he told her gently, "If you're sure you're all right, then I'll go." But he didn't move an inch; he continued to stand there and look at her.

Of course I'm not all right! she screeched at him

silently. *Can't you see that I'm bleeding on the inside. That I need you so desperately!* She had tried to banish Linc from her mind and her soul. What a complete imbecile she was to think she could!

Suddenly, she realized that she loved him and wanted him no matter what he did for a living. He could play football for the rest of his life if that was what he chose to do. It was no longer important. She realized that she had made a grave error in trying to change him. It was imperative that she accept him the way he was. That was what Linc had been trying to tell her all along. But she had been so wrapped up in her own selfish desires that she hadn't seen it.

Keeley felt sure he hadn't come to this room to make amends. It was probably a twinge of concern that had prodded him to seek her out. After all, hadn't she fainted for the second time right in front of his eyes? That in itself had been enough to pique his curiosity.

He no longer loved her. Of that she was sure. But she loved him. She had come full circle from attraction to alienation, and finally to committed love and devotion. Linc was part of her now. As much a part of her as the baby she would bear.

The baby! Their baby. Suddenly, she knew beyond a shadow of a doubt that if she told Linc about the baby, he would marry her tomorrow. Could she tell him? Could she trap him that way? *No!* She rebelled against doing that, not only for his sake but hers as well. It went against every principle she held near and dear to her.

But it wouldn't have worked anyway, she told herself with a punishing honesty. She had made such a big deal out of not being on the birth control pill, and then she'd gotten pregnant. It reeked of entrapment! It wasn't fair to him. She could never live with herself if she backed him into that corner. Never.

If only she could have another chance....

Suddenly, without warning, the door to the bedroom opened, shattering the silence in the room.

Keeley swung around to find Jim confronting her with worry etched deeply into the lines of his face. "Damn, Keeley," he groaned. "I've been half out of my mind! Are you—" He stopped and took in first the deadly pallor of her skin and then turned and saw Linc.

A thick silence fell over the room.

Jim, with the protective instinct of a mother with her young pups, quickly closed the gap between him and Keeley. Completely ignoring Linc, he put his arm around her waist. "Honey, let me take you home," he offered in a gentle voice.

Keeley died a thousand times over as Linc's next words ripped through her brain with the same destructive force as a ball slamming through a glass door.

"I see that nothing has changed." Linc then swung on his heel and walked through the door, not even bothering to close it behind him.

Keeley stood transfixed and stared through the empty door. Linc's exit had created a dark void in her life. This time, she was certain it was forever.

She couldn't even cry as Jim led her to the bed and all but forced her to sit on the edge of it. He knelt down in front of her, clasping her cold, numb hands within his and rubbing them.

"Keeley," he demanded, "what did Hunter say to you to put that look of sudden death in your eyes? It took all my willpower to keep from putting my fist through that 'pretty boy' face of his. All you have to do is say the word and I'll be after him faster than a cat after a canary.''

Jim's vow to go after Linc was enough to bring Keeley swiftly out of her pain-riddled stupor. The offer was so out of character for Jim that it frightened her. He meant every word he had said. The hard coldness of his usually warm eyes bore that out.

"Jim," Keeley whispered desperately, "you must promise me you won't do anything or say anything to Linc. Promise me!"

Jim frowned and then sighed deeply. "All right. I'll give you my word if it means that much to you. But don't you think you owe me some type of explanation?"

"Now?"

"Yes, now. This minute."

Keeley gestured tiredly. "It'll have to wait, Jim. I must try to get through this wedding. But when we get to my apartment, we'll talk. I promise," she declared in a tone that held both weariness and firm conviction.

"Pregnant!"

Keeley's stomach turned a somersault as she stood in her apartment and faced an irate Jim.

"I don't believe you!" he screeched, his face deathly white.

"It—it's true," Keeley whispered as she tried to look away from his glowering countenance.

Her promise to Jim was the last thing she had remembered with any clarity after she had recovered from her fainting spell, other than insisting that she was able to take part in the brief ceremony as planned.

As quickly and unobtrusively as possible she had assured her father and Judith that she was fine and that she didn't blame them for Linc's presence. They both had assured her that they had no idea that he was coming. She believed them.

The moment the minister had pronounced an ecstatic Luther and Judith husband and wife, the party broke out in full swing. She had done everything in her power to leave the moment the ceremony ended, but all her efforts failed.

At twelve o'clock in the morning, she found it virtually impossible to use any finesse in telling Jim the truth. Before she realized it, she had blurted out her condition to him.

"Jim, I'm so sorry," she whispered. "Sorry I—I betrayed you."

"Sorry!" he bit out savagely. "Is that all you have to say for carrying another man's seed inside you while still engaged to me?"

"Don't, please—" she pleaded softly as huge tears ran down her cheeks. "I didn't mean to hurt you."

"Like hell you didn't," he countered swiftly. "If that was the case, you wouldn't have gotten yourself pregnant by Mr. Super Stud. God, how could you?"

"Because *I love him!*" she retaliated, sobs now raking her slim body. Unknowingly she again splayed her hand across her stomach as if to protect her baby from all the verbal abuse.

Following her outburst, there was silence in the room, broken only by the sobs that continued to shake her body.

Suddenly Jim's shoulders sagged in defeat. With a groan he covered the space between them and gently folded Keeley within his arms.

"Shhh," he murmured as he patted first her head and then her back, trying to get her to stop crying. "You'll make yourself sick."

Gently he propelled her toward the couch and lowered her into its soft cushions. He pulled a handkerchief from his hip pocket and gave it to her.

Finally Keeley was able to push back the sobs that held a stranglehold on her throat.

They stared at each other in painful silence for a long moment.

"When are you getting married?" he asked at length.

"I'm not." There was no reason to run from the truth. It had to be faced—now was as good a time as any, she told herself. She couldn't further insult Jim with anything less than the truth.

He shot her an incredulous look before jumping up from the couch and pacing the floor in front of her. His usual calm facade was cracked. He was upset and it showed.

Suddenly he stopped and peered closely at her. His dark eyes were dangerously slanted. "Won't that bas—" He paused and cleared his throat. "Won't Hunter marry you?"

"He—he doesn't know about the baby." Would the evening ever end? she wondered in hopeless despair.

"Damn it, Keeley, what kind of game are you playing?"

Tears streamed down her face again as she met his outraged eyes. "Believe me, it's no game. I've never been more serious in my entire life."

"Are you going to keep the baby?"

"You should know the answer to that question al-

242   *Mary Lynn Baxter*

ready. I've lost one baby; I couldn't handle losing this one. It's—it's my reason for living,'' she added, her voice an aching whisper.

Jim sat down beside her and reached for her hand. "I won't lie to you and pretend that I understand why you chose to do this to yourself. But I want you to know that I still love you, even though my behavior of a few minutes ago didn't show it. And I'd marry you tomorrow if you'd just say the word.''

"Jim—''

"No, let me finish, please. All I'm asking from you now is a promise that if you need me for any reason, you'll call me.''

"I—I promise.'' But she wouldn't call him. He knew it. She knew it. There was no substitute for Linc. Buried deep within her lay the only hope for her future.

Keeley battled against the raw January wind as it tore through her with billowing force. Of all times to fumble with her keys, she thought with impatience. Finally able to get the door open, she went immediately to the dining room table, where she dumped her armload of ungraded papers.

She then collapsed into the nearest chair and fought for her breath, exhausted. At this rate, she wouldn't be able to continue to work much longer. The doctor had warned her about pushing herself too hard and becoming overtired. She had to think about the baby, he had cautioned, even if she didn't care about herself.

Since day one of her move back to her apartment in Eugene, a cold, dark loneliness had haunted her with avid persistence. During the last month her work at the university had been rewarding. Jim had become a staunch friend and ally, for which she was grateful. Her father and Judith were extremely happy, and she no longer had to worry about Luther's health, which had improved.

The Timberjacks had won the Super Bowl, and Luther was still high as a kite over the victory. He and Stan had even patched up their differences. A smile appeared briefly across her stiff features now as she thought about all the backslapping and congratulations that had taken place between the two men. They had been like eager kids, ready to forgive and forget. She was proud, too, that Luther's dream had come true. The victory had definitely lifted the team out of its financial woes. She *should* have been content.

Instead she was miserable. Thoughts of Linc had continued to plague her day and night. This evening was no exception. She wondered if he was happy, if he was pleased with the million-dollar contract that Luther had offered him. Immediately following the Super Bowl win, the papers had been full of Linc's pictures along with stories about his contract negotiations.

If only things had been different.

Let it go! Don't torture yourself this way!

Deciding that even her panties and bra were now an encumbrance to her swelling stomach, she removed them along with her dress. Due to her slender physique and finely knit bones, it was already obvious that she was pregnant.

Smiling, she stared at her naked body and placed a hand on her stomach. Four months pregnant and she was already showing! She wouldn't be able to keep her condition from her father much longer, she thought, with a grimness now replacing her smile.

She put on her long flannel robe with matching slippers and padded into the kitchen.

Food tasted like cardboard in her mouth, but she forced herself to eat every bite of her dinner. After cleaning up the kitchen, she settled herself comfortably on the couch. The next project for the evening was to grade papers. She had put the first red mark on the paper when the doorbell rang.

Exasperated, she laid the pen and paper aside and ambled toward the door. Positive her visitor was simply a neighbor wanting to borrow something, she flipped the deadbolt lock and opened the door.

Linc was standing on the threshold. His hands were jammed in his pockets of his windbreaker to ward off the stubborn chill of the night air.

He pushed past her before she had a chance to open her mouth. "A body could freeze to death waiting for you to get to the door," he said lightly. "And do you always open the door without first asking who's there?" he added, a frown further aggravating his haggard features.

"What—what are you doing here?" she gasped, completely ignoring his outburst concerning the door.

She was dry-mouthed and nervous as her gaze darted up at him. From where he stood she saw that her first assessment of his condition was correct. His face was indeed haggard and thin. The sight of it, reflected in the bright light of the room, was almost her undoing.

Where was the happy and excited person she had imagined him to be? Whatever he was feeling, it certainly wasn't happiness. It seemed as if every ounce of extra flesh was gone from his cheeks, and his eyes looked strained to the limit with red streaks running through them. Yet they were burning with brilliance and intensity as they looked at her from his position in the center of the room.

Keeley held on to her sanity by a thread as she returned his dark and penetrating stare. She watched as his expression changed from one of hostility to one of hot, burning passion that set her soul on fire.

"Keeley!"

His cry straight from the edge of hell set her weak knees into motion. She crossed the room and stood in front of the fireplace, turning her back to him. She waited with her heart in her throat.

She didn't have to turn around to know he was there. His fragrance fanned her senses and sent them flowing like a gurgling mountain spring on a sunny day.

Before she could move, speak or *think,* his hand reached around her waist and loosened the casually looped tie that held her robe together.

It was a toss-up as to which one of their harshly indrawn breaths was the loudest as Linc's callused fingers made contact with the alluring softness of her bare skin.

Keeley almost strangled as she tried to hold back the sob that gurgled in her throat. She needed strength to endure the skillful pilgrimage of his fingers as they roamed with thorough slowness over the protruding softness of her lower body.

When his fingers brushed against the golden gateway that had become awakened by his touch and his touch only, she gasped aloud and leaned her head back against the solid wall of his chest. Silent agony, laced with sweet rapture, rippled through her body like the taste of a dry white wine when it hit the tongue.

Please! I can't take much more!

But her silent plea went unheeded. Leaving her rounded stomach, his hand caressed its way upward to surround the satin fullness of her breasts. She heard his heart pound with ever-increasing vigor as his fingers caught a nipple, already peaked to budding hardness.

She came close to fainting again as his other hand joined in the pleasure by cupping the other breast and treating it to the same gentle pleasure.

"Keeley, oh, Keeley," he whispered with devastating anguish in his voice, "weren't you even going to tell me?"

Suddenly, sobs tore through her body as she turned around and burrowed her face against the warm hardness of his body.

For a timeless moment, Linc held her close to his heart, letting her tears run their course.

Slowly she lifted shimmering bright eyes to look into his tormented face. "Do you—you hate me?" It was difficult to squeeze the words through her tight throat, but Linc heard them.

A sigh shook his body. "When I first realized that you were carrying my child—" He stopped short and looked down into Keeley's face. There was no need to voice the question.

"Of course it's your child," she volunteered.

His body seemed to turn to liquid putty before he went on. "I wanted to strangle you with my bare hands." He paused again and swallowed convulsively. "But when my hand touched the velvet of your naked skin, I wanted only to get down on my knees and beg you to forgive me for sending you away. Keeley, will you give me another chance?''

"Oh, Linc, Linc," she cried, "tell me I'm not dreaming all this." Her hands were busy touching the gaunt shadows in his face as if to prove to herself that he wasn't a mirage.

"Oh, my love, I'm real," he promised with a heart-stopping smile curving his lips. "And I intend to show you just how real."

Before his words penetrated Keeley's brain, he swept her up in his arms and made his way with his precious burden into the bedroom. He carefully laid her down on the bed, drenched in a muted glow pouring from the full moon that proudly danced in the heavens.

Clothes were quickly disposed of in their efforts to come together in consoling sweetness. The mattress sank as Linc laid his body next to hers.

His mouth sought and latched onto the moist heat of hers. As his lips plundered hers in electric urgency his hands were circling her body, creating the same feeling everywhere he touched.

"Keeley," he groaned, pulling his lips away from hers, "I don't want to hurt you, but I want you so—"

"You won't hurt me," she assured him as she twined her legs around his upper thighs. She immediately began to rub the soft cheeks of his buttocks with the heels of her feet.

"Keeley...Keeley...Keeley, ah...yes...feels so good...so right."

Linc's mouth then searched for Keeley's as her tender kneading brought his manly swell to throbbing readiness.

Instantly she arched against him, opening herself to receive all of him with an ardor that matched his own.

As they moved together through a seemingly endless tunnel of shared pleasure, deep and intense, Keeley felt her soul leave her body and enter his.

In that precise moment, she got a glimpse of eternity, as they became one in a perfectly attuned and coordinated culmination of shared ecstasy.

Keeley awakened with a languor that rendered her limbs heavy, unmovable. She felt as if hot needles were pricking her skin. Blinking her eyes several times, she finally pinpointed the reason for her awareness.

Linc's mouth was bestowing gentle nipping kisses on her swelling stomach. Noticing her slight movement, he raised his head and looked at her.

"How old is our baby?" he asked.

Keeley smiled. "About four months now."

"Kee—ley," his voice broke. When he could speak again he said, with his heart in his eyes, "I love you."

"And I love you," she returned simply.

He moved up and turned Keeley so that she was cradled within his arms. "Will you marry me?"

"Is tomorrow too soon?"

A deep laugh shook his frame as he rocked her in his arms and then patted her behind lovingly.

"I can see we're going to have a marriage made in heaven, you insatiable wench." His eyes were glowing with love.

There was a moment of strained silence as Keeley pondered the best way to say she was sorry.

"Linc—"

"Yes, love," he murmured.

"About—about football."

She felt him tense. "What about football?"

"I—I just want you to know that I don't care if you play football or what you do. I—I know now how wrong it was for me to try and change you."

He remained silent for a moment as he brushed soft tendrils away from Keeley's face. "Thank you for saying that, my love. But I too have a confession to make. I came by with the intention of saying goodbye to you." Keeley pulled away from Linc and stared at him with puzzled eyes.

"You heard me right. I didn't sign my contract." Ignoring her gasp, he continued, "After I lost you, nothing was the same. Somehow I managed to put myself back together enough to do my part to win the Super Bowl." He smiled. "And I did that for you and Luther. I knew about his problems with the team and the pressure that he was under, so I did my best to help him out."

Before he could say any more, Keeley sealed her lips to his.

There was another silence.

Laughing, they soon broke apart, breathless and achingly aroused again, but they both knew how important it was to rid themselves of all the dark moments that had plagued their past so as not to mar their future.

"Linc," Keeley whispered, "are you sure that's what you want to do? Give up football, I mean?"

He grazed her cheek with his lips. "Next to you and the baby, I want that more than anything else in the world."

"I'm—I'm glad you want the baby."

"How could I not? It's the very best of both of us. How can he go wrong?" He laughed at his own swelled pride. "By the way," he added, "how does Luther feel about the baby?"

Keeley paled. "He—he doesn't know yet."

"Good," Linc countered brightly. "Tomorrow after I put my ring on your finger, we'll tell him together. How does that sound to you?"

"Marvelous," she said with shining eyes. "Dad will be beside himself with excitement." Then her eyes clouded immediately. "How did he take it when you refused to sign your contract?" She hated to hear the answer and have her perfect day filled with shadows.

Linc's lip twitched. "Well, I'd say he took it rather well after he told me what a damn fool I was for letting you go in the first place."

An incredulous look crossed Keeley's face. "Linc! I don't believe you!"

"It's the truth, I swear it. He turned me every which way but loose with his scolding. Told me exactly what he'd do to me if I ever mistreated you."

"Oh, Linc—"

"But I was still afraid to approach you. Afraid you'd spit in my face. And when you fainted again at the wedding, I promised myself I'd leave you alone."

"What changed your mind?" she asked softly.

He thought for a moment. "There was something different about you that day. Your body seemed fuller. And your breasts! God, how they called to me, lured me." He paused and cleared his throat. "But I still didn't put two and two together until I walked in here tonight and saw you.''

''Are you sure I'm forgiven for almost throwing it all away?''

He bent down and brushed his lips against hers. ''Without you, I wouldn't want to continue living.''

Keeley cradled his face within her hand. ''You awakened me with your first touch and made me alive,'' she whispered, her breath warm as it fluttered across his face. ''And I want you to remember always that you *are* my life.''

Don't miss this chance to get these popular titles
from *New York Times* bestselling author

BARBARA DELINSKY

RACHEL

C A U G H T

LEE

...in a web of danger.

Kate Devane is being
stalked on the Internet
by someone who knows
too much about her;
Connor Quinn is being
manipulated by a serial
killer. Can they trust
each other...if only to
escape the terror of a
madman's web?

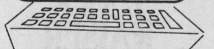

A story of romantic suspense by the bestselling author of
A FATEFUL CHOICE.

Get **CAUGHT** this November 1997
at your favorite retail outlet.

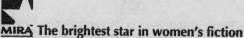

MIRA The brightest star in women's fiction

**A showgirl, a minister—
and an unsolved murder.**

EASY VIRTUE

Eight years ago Mary Margaret's father was
convicted of a violent murder she knew he
didn't commit—and she vowed to clear his
name. With her father serving a life sentence,
Mary Margaret is working as a showgirl in Reno
when Reverend Dane Barrett shows up with
information about her father's case. Working to
expose the real killer, the unlikely pair also
proceed to expose themselves to an unknown
enemy who is intent on keeping the past buried.

**From the bestselling author of
LAST NIGHT IN RIO**

JANICE
KAISER

Available in December 1997
at your favorite retail outlet.

MIRA
BOOKS

The Brightest Stars in Women's Fiction.™

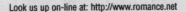

Indiscreet

Camilla Ferrand wants everyone, especially her dying
grandfather, to stop worrying about her. So she tells
them that she is engaged to be married. But with no
future husband in sight, it's going to be difficult to
keep up the pretense. Then she meets the very
handsome and mysterious Benedict Ellsworth who
generously offers to accompany Camilla to her
family's estate—as her most devoted fiancé.

But at what cost does this *generosity* come?

From the bestselling author of *Impulse*

Candace Camp

Available in November 1997
at your favorite retail outlet.

"Candace Camp also writes for Silhouette® as Kristen James